Intimate Enemy
MARILYN PAPPANO

MILLS & BOON

First published in Great Britain 2009
Large Print edition 2009
Harlequin Mills & Boon Limited,
Eton House, 18-24 Paradise Road,
Richmond, Surrey TW9 1SR

© Marilyn Pappano 2008

ISBN: 978 0 263 21016 3

Set in Times Roman 17¼ on 20 pt.
35-1209-60843

Harlequin Mills & Boon policy is to use papers that
are natural, renewable and recyclable products and
made from wood grown in sustainable forests. The
logging and manufacturing process conform to the legal
environmental regulations of the country of origin.

Printed and bound in Great Britain
by CPI Antony Rowe, Chippenham, Wiltshire

MARILYN PAPPANO

brings impeccable credentials to her career—a lifelong habit of gazing out of windows, not paying attention in class, daydreaming and spinning tales for her own entertainment. The sale of her first book brought great relief to her family, proving that she wasn't crazy but was, instead, creative. Since then she's sold more than forty books to various publishers and even a film production company.

She writes in an office nestled among the oaks that surround her home. In winter she stays inside with her husband and their four dogs, and in summer she spends her free time mowing the yard that never stops growing and daydreams about grass that never gets taller than two inches. You can write to her at PO Box 642, Sapulpa, OK 74067-0643, USA.

For the Smart Women
of Romance Writers Ink, the
best writers, support and friends ever,
You guys rule!

Chapter 1

In a small town like Copper Lake, Georgia, there were benefits to having an office right on the square, Jamie Munroe thought as she gazed out the window behind her desk. These days, there were bigger benefits being on the corner just off the square. Namely, the mega-construction project going on across the street, turning a shabby, rundown apartment building back into the gracious pre-war gem it had once been.

Okay, so the noise and traffic could be a hassle, but the workers…

"I swear, the best-looking guys in the county are on this crew," she murmured.

A few feet away, Lys Paxton, paralegal, computer wiz and friend, *uh-huh*ed with her feet propped on the credenza, her gaze locked on a pair of the smoothest, tannest, strongest, sexiest backs—and backsides—Jamie had ever seen. Both men wore jeans, faded, snug and caked with the usual residue of construction work, and both had stripped off their shirts in deference to the morning heat. They were unloading lumber from the bed of a pickup, and they were definitely ogle-worthy.

Lys sighed, her hands clasped loosely around a cold can of diet pop. "Don't you love it when the lumberyard can't make deliveries on short notice?"

"Hmm. Remind me to send the owner my thanks."

It was ten-thirty on Wednesday morning, and Jamie and Lys were officially on a coffee break. Up until a few weeks ago they'd actually locked up the office and walked over to the coffee shop on the square to spend ten bucks and fifteen minutes relaxing. Then the work had started on the mansion, and they'd begun taking their breaks in the office, chairs turned to the window, feet up, savoring.

It was the only male-female relationship of any sort in Jamie's life these days. Pathetic.

"When was the last time you went on a date?" Lys asked.

"I don't remember."

"Me, either." Another sigh. "I need one. Bad."

Jamie hadn't *needed* a man in a long time, not since law school, and she didn't intend to let it happen again. Oh, she wasn't giving them up or anything. She could want and have. She could use and discard. She could have a perfectly normal relationship. She would just never let herself *need* a man.

Men were dangerous to a woman's health. Every woman she knew had gotten her heart broken, her faith shaken and her self-esteem smacked. A couple of them had lost all their money to the rat bastards, as well.

Using, enjoying, not trusting, not needing. That was the way to go.

"I call the guy on the right with the rip in his jeans beneath his truly impressive butt," Lys said.

"You're welcome to him. I'll take the one on the left. I like a man who saves his revealing clothes for just me."

"Okay, it's time for them to turn around. The mystery faces revealed. Think we know either of them?"

"If I do, I haven't seen them like that before." Not that she made a particular habit of looking at men's butts.

When the last board was in place, both men did turn, Lys's first. He was as hot from the front as from the back, and unfamiliar to them both. Jamie's pick was slower. He bent to retrieve a bottle of water from the cooler next to his booted feet before straightening, giving them an oblique view as he tipped his head back and drained half the water at once. Watching his fingers grip the bottle, his throat work to swallow, his muscles ripple from the relief of the cold water, Jamie suddenly felt as if her own temperature had redlined. She was groping for her pop on the desk and found it just as he turned to face the window head-on.

The pop fell over, dripping off the desk to puddle on the mat. Lys choked, coughing until she sputtered, and Jamie turned to pure ice inside, too frozen to move or think.

Russ Calloway, owner of Calloway Construction. Brother to her good friend, Robbie. Respondent in the first divorce case she'd handled after coming to town. Sworn enemy. Former lover.

"Son of a bitch." Lys grabbed a handful of tissues to blot the desk pad, then mop up the cola on the floor. Catching Jamie's chair, she spun it around so her back was to the street. "There should be a warning."

Jamie managed a faint smile. "The signs on

all those trucks over there do say Calloway Construction. So does the big fancy sign the bank put up at the corner." *This Calloway Construction Project Is Funded By Fidelity Mutual Of Copper Lake.*

"Yeah, but he's the freakin' boss. He's not supposed to be over there."

He was a hands-on boss, by all accounts. Just because they hadn't seen him before didn't mean he wouldn't show up. The crew had been working for only two weeks, doing basic demolition. She'd known he would be on site eventually. She'd been prepared for it. Eventually.

"It's not like I don't ever see him around town," she said, reassuring herself as much as Lys. "A woman can get lost pretty easily among twenty-thousand people, but there's always that chance."

"Yeah, but you don't drool over him if you catch a glimpse of him at the grocery store, do you?"

"Of course not," Jamie said. Truth was, she did. She couldn't remember a single time in her life when she hadn't felt at least a faint stirring of lust for Russ. Not when he'd broken up with her, not when he'd broken her heart, not when he'd sat in the conference room with her and his soon-to-be ex looking as if he despised them both.

It was his loss, Robbie had told her the one time she'd cried on his shoulder. Russ was being an ass—and Robbie knew, being the undisputed official ass of the Calloway family.

If it was his loss, why did it hurt *her?*

"Stop it!" Lys admonished. "I can tell by the look in your eyes, you're still thinking about him."

"Actually, I was thinking about that contract I have to negotiate with Robbie in ten minutes," she lied, forcing herself to really think about it. "He's such a phony—makes everyone think he's lazy and shallow and doesn't care about anything but fun, when he's a damn good lawyer."

"Which doesn't negate the fact that he really is lazy and shallow." Lys separated the Andersen folder from the stack on Jamie's desk and handed it to her. "He's a classic Calloway. They're all worthless with the exception of Sara, and she wasn't born into the family. She only married into it and had the sense to stick around and enjoy the benefits after her scum husband died."

Jamie slid the folder into her bag, easily mistaken for an attaché. What could she say? She loved big purses. She was prepared for anything.

Except finding out that the man she was lusting over was Russ.

"Your meeting with Robbie is at the country club at eleven," Lys said, "and then you're supposed to see the shrink in Augusta about Laurie Stinson. He's expecting you at two. And since he charges by the hour, he'll probably be quite wordy, so you should go on home when you get back. I'll close up here."

"Robbie switched lunch to that new little place on the river—Chantal's. Says he's had all the country-club food he can stomach for a while." Jamie slipped off her sweater and folded it over her arm. The restaurant would probably be cold, but the four-block walk over wouldn't. "And I'll be back. I'll want to make notes on this afternoon's interview. But don't you wait around. I may have dinner in Augusta first."

Halfway to the door, she turned back. "Thanks a bunch, Lys. I don't know what I'd do without you."

"You'd probably still be sharing office space with Robbie and getting nothing done." Lys went into the outer office and settled in at her desk. "Have fun, boss."

Jamie went out the door and into the foyer. She was not, was *not* going to look across the street when she stepped out. She would turn left, walk the fifty feet to the corner, then turn left again. That was all.

She opened the door, stepped outside into the

muggy May heat and her gaze zinged in on the construction site so fast that her vision went blurry. Lys's hunk was still there, and so was Russ. He leaned against the lowered tailgate of the truck, legs stretched out, ankles crossed, and they were talking. If she tried, she could hear his voice. The street wasn't that wide, the midday noises not that loud.

But she didn't try. She put on a pair of over-sized sunglasses that hid half her face, turned left, bypassed her car and reached the corner without really being aware of the journey. Once she'd turned and solid limestone blocked the site from view, she sighed, her shoulders relaxing.

She'd known it wouldn't be easy living in the town Russ's family had founded and still pretty much owned two hundred years later. She hadn't expected easy. She just hadn't known it could be this hard.

Copper Lake was a lovely town, designed with aesthetics in mind. The entire downtown was on the historic register, where codes were rigid, and even new construction in town was closely monitored. The newest neighborhoods were almost as charming as the oldest, and even the shopping mall fit into the town planners' view for it.

She passed the square, site of war monuments, political rallies and summer-evening concerts. After crossing River Road, she took a few steps down into Calloway Construction's recently completed riverside retail complex. It was beautiful, looked as if it had been there a hundred years, and was already at full occupancy only a month after opening. Idly she wondered how much was Russ's vision and how much had come from his architects and designers. It was hard to think of him and *charming* in the same thought. Even before he'd hated her, he hadn't been exactly charming. Blunt, forthright, not charming.

She located Chantal's in the corner, and the hostess showed her to a covered deck with paddle fans cooling the air. Robbie was seated at a table near the river, gazing out as if he'd rather be out there fishing in his john boat than working.

She nudged his shoulder before setting her sweater and bag in the seat across from him. He wore jeans, honest-to-God pressed and creased, deck shoes and a polo shirt in bright lemon-yellow. Every other lawyer in town wore suits to work, but not him. He didn't even wear them to court unless he was feeling generous. Clothes didn't make a bad case good or turn a good one bad, he said. It didn't hurt that he was a Calloway, and a good lawyer.

"Hey, babe." He stood and kissed her cheek, then held the chair for her. "You walked over here, didn't you? If you'd called, I would have picked you up."

"If I'd wanted a ride, I would have driven. How are you?"

"Anticipating my vacation. Tomorrow morning, six-fifteen, I'm on a plane to Miami."

She'd heard all about the trip. A leisurely

drive halfway through the Keys, then seven days on one of the charter fishing boats owned by a law school classmate. A fishing pole, beer and sun—all a Calloway needed to be happy. "Have fun."

"It's not too late for you to join me."

He'd made the offer before; she declined again. "Fishing isn't my idea of a vacation."

"Your loss. Anything new on—?" He shrugged.

She smiled politely at the waitress who set a glass of ice water in front of her, then made a face at Robbie. "I managed to forget it all morning, and now you bring it up."

His scowl reminded her of his brothers, any and all of them. Gerald Calloway had had four sons, three with his wife and one with a girl-friend. Rick, Russ and Robbie, along with Mitch Lassiter, second in the lineup, all bore a very strong resemblance. Dark hair, dark skin, startlingly blue eyes, voices that sounded similar and matching scowls. Rick was the handsomest, Jamie had long ago decided, Mitch the most mysterious, Robbie the most charming and Russ the sexiest.

"You've got a freakin' stalker, Jamie. You shouldn't be forgetting it."

His words chased away what little ease she'd recovered after seeing Russ. *Stalker*—it sounded so ugly that she avoided using the word to describe the mystery man who'd come into her life a few weeks earlier. Secret admirer sounded so much more harmless. Less deadly.

Less likely, logic forced her to admit. But she'd lived through a nightmare before. She preferred the state of denial at this point.

"The flowers were the last thing." A dozen apricot roses—her favorite—waiting in a vase on her steps when she'd gotten home Monday evening.

"What the hell kind of guy sends apricot roses?" Robbie asked. "Red, yellow, pink—those are guy roses. You can't even buy apricot roses in Copper Lake. They're a special order thing."

She smiled faintly. "You called the florists, too?"

"Of course. And none of them had gotten an order for apricot roses in months. Did you call the police?"

"And say what? Someone sent me flowers? Left a note on my windshield? Had a box of chocolates delivered to my office? It's a little creepy, Robbie, but the guy hasn't crossed the line."

"Yet."

"Gee, thanks. That makes me feel better."

"Jamie—"

She pulled the file from her bag. "I've got to be in Augusta in a few hours. We should work while we eat."

He looked as if he wanted to protest, but after a moment his mouth flattened. "Okay. But next thing that happens, if you don't call the police, I do. Agreed?"

Jamie knew he wasn't kidding. His best bud was a detective with the Copper Lake Police Department, Rick worked for the Georgia Bureau of Investigation and Mitch worked for the state BI in Mississippi.

"Agreed."

Not that anything else was going to happen. Her admirer was shy but harmless. She wanted to believe that. Needed to, for her own peace of mind.

When his cell phone rang, Russ Calloway seriously considered not answering. He received about fifty calls a day, and at least forty-nine of them were complaints. He wasn't betting that this one would be the exception.

Still, he fished the phone from his pocket and flipped it open. "This is Calloway."

"Hey, so is this." Robbie, kid brother, company lawyer and eternal pain in the butt.

"What's up?" Russ asked absently, phone braced between his ear and shoulder while he examined the framing around a third-floor door.

"The price of gas. The price of a good time."

"You've been talking to Mitch." Those were their older brother's stock answers to the question. "How is he?"

"Anxious for this kid to be born."

"Jessica still turning on a dime?"

"If she's not puking, she's bitching. Mitch is pretty much afraid to be around her. Seems like the morning sickness and the hormones are all his fault."

"The joys of impending fatherhood," Russ said dryly. The segment of trim was nearly five feet long and looked in good enough shape to survive the prying experience, once he got the nails loosened. "Hang on," he muttered, then sorted through the tools on the worktable until he found a hammer, a screwdriver and pry bars of varying sizes.

"Jeez, you can't even stop for two minutes for a phone call?" Robbie complained.

See? Russ had known this call wasn't going to be the exception. "Some of us work for a living."

"Yeah, but you overdo it. I bet you haven't even taken a break for lunch, have you?"

Russ glanced at his watch. It was nearly two. "Not yet. And I bet you have. A couple of hours. With a pretty woman."

"It was a working lunch, and it didn't come close to two hours. But you're right about the woman. She's gorgeous."

Hearing about the women in his brothers' lives was about as close to a relationship as Russ got these days. Considering that Rick and Mitch were both married, that left only Robbie for any real variety. Good thing he didn't limit himself to a type. "Who is this living, breathing goddess?"

"Jamie."

Robbie said more—he always did—but Russ quit listening. His gut clenched, and his jaw tightened until he felt real pain. Jamie Munroe was the one sore point between him and his brother. Robbie thought she was the perfect woman, and Russ wouldn't piss on her if she was on fire. He'd spent a lot of time wishing she would disappear off the face of the earth.

But she'd made herself at home in his hometown and showed no signs of leaving, so he'd learned to ignore her. It worked pretty well until he caught a glimpse of her on the sidewalk or going into the courthouse or browsing through the fruit at the farmer's market. When he wasn't prepared to see her, it was always a surprise. Recognition, an instant of normalcy, remembering old friends, law school, getting married. Then came the scorn.

Pry bar resting two inches under the molding, Russ realized Robbie was waiting for him to say something. His fingers throbbed from holding the tool so tightly, never a good sign when working with two-hundred-year-old wood, so he set it aside. Holding the phone in one hand, he tilted his head the other way to rub the ache in his neck. "What'd you say?"

"I said even you can't argue the fact that she's pretty."

Jamie? Pretty? Brown hair, light gold skin, a few freckles, blue eyes. Yeah, he supposed she was pretty, if a man liked the backstabbing viper type.

"Of course I can argue," he replied. "Don't forget, I've seen her with her fangs and cape."

"Aw, come on, bubba. It's been three years. Quit holding a grudge because the better lawyer won."

Correction: There was more than one sore point between them. Robbie thought the divorce was something Russ should have put behind him the day it was over. He thought Russ should acknowledge that he'd been an idiot to represent himself, that Jamie was better and get on with life.

Hell, he knew she was a better lawyer than him. He'd gone through school with the knowledge that he wasn't ever going to practice; once he'd taken and passed the bar, that was the end of it for him. She damn well should be better.

And he knew he'd been an idiot to represent himself, law degree or no. Robbie had wanted to take over, had all but bounced in the air, shouting, "Let me, let me!" And his brother wouldn't have let anything get in the way of getting the best deal for his client. Melinda might have been his sister-in-law and Jamie his best friend, but he would have trampled them both into the dirt to win.

Russ's marriage had been the most important thing in his life. Facing a divorce had been bad enough. Finding out about Melinda's affairs, her scorn for him and her lies had been damn near unbearable. Add to that, Jamie, once his own friend, allowing—encouraging?—Melinda's deceit… He'd gone from love for one and friendship with the other to despising them both.

He was over the divorce. He'd gotten on with his life. But he wasn't the forgive-and-forget type. His motto was: live and learn, and never give 'em a chance to screw you twice.

"Did you call for a reason?" he asked testily. "Because I've got about four more hours of work before I get out of here, and shooting the breeze with you isn't getting it done."

"Man, you need to get laid. You're getting pissier every day. I did call for a reason. Mom's been trying to get hold of you, but she keeps getting your voice mail. Rick and Amanda are coming over Saturday, and she wants you there for dinner. Seven o'clock, no grubby work clothes, and if you want to bring a date, she wouldn't object."

"Yeah, Saturday at seven. I'll be there." Before Robbie could say anything else, Russ hung up.

If he wanted to bring a date... He hadn't been out on a date in more than six years, since he'd married Melinda, and hadn't had sex in about three years, since she'd thrown him out.

His brothers could understand his not dating—they'd all gotten screwed over at some point—but no sex… Hell, even his mother would wonder about that.

It wasn't that he wasn't interested. It was the intimacy he didn't want, and he'd forgotten how to separate the two. He'd once known—in high school, in college and law school. He'd always had a girlfriend or two, and while the sex had been fun, it had never really meant anything.

Finding out that sex meant nothing to the wife he'd loved had somehow made it mean too much to him. Was that twisted or what?

Frustrated, he walked to one of the arched windows that faced west in what had been the third-floor ballroom of River's Edge, a classic Greek Revival plantation home. It had once reigned over eight thousand acres until a long-gone Calloway had decided it was the perfect place to build his legacy. He'd bought the property, torn down everything except the house itself and made it his home while building the town around it. He'd decreed that no building between the house and the river could be higher than two stories to preserve the view from the third floor. Russ could see the Gullah River, a hundred yards wide at this point, as well as a dozen or more of his projects, old and new.

He'd always wanted to go into construction, even though Calloway men were lawyers whether they practiced or not. Rick had been the first to break tradition, getting his degree in criminal justice instead. Russ hadn't followed his lead, but had gone to the University of Georgia School of Law like a good Calloway son. It would make the family happy, he'd figured, and with his entire life ahead of him, a few years in law school couldn't hurt, right?

Yeah, right. He'd met Jamie there, which had led to meeting Melinda. The bloodsucker and the bitch.

Speak of the devil, or, at least, one of

them…Jamie came out of her office across the street. Her hair was pulled back and clipped up in kind of a mess on the back of her head. She wore a red-and-white print dress that didn't reach her knees, with a sweater that was more for looks than warmth, and she carried a brief-case and a bottle of water. Huge dark glasses covered her eyes, but he could tell she never looked toward the house before she slid behind the wheel of her character-free black convertible.

He watched her back out from the space in front of her office, then drive off to the south. If he had any luck, she would keep driving south until she wound up somewhere deep in the Gulf of Mexico. But at the end of the block, she turned, jogged over to River Road, then headed north.

"Staring out the window doesn't get the work done."

He turned to find J. D. Stinson standing at the top of what had once been elegant stairs. They'd been chopped up along with the rest of the house sometime in the fifties, turning the place into cheap apartment rentals.

J.D. was a relative, too; his mother was Russ's father's youngest sister. He was an assistant vice president at Fidelity and oversaw all of Russ's construction loans. Nothing like keeping it in the family.

"I always finish ahead of schedule and under budget," Russ said mildly.

"And you usually have bonuses for doing so written into your contract."

Russ shrugged. He had a reputation for doing good work at a fair price. If people were willing to pay him extra for doing it quickly, as well, why not? "What are you doing out of the office and on the site on a warm day like today?"

It was a family joke that J.D. had gone into banking not because his father was president and it was expected of him, but because it meant an air-conditioned job wearing nice clothes. Casual for him was khakis and a polo shirt. He owned more suits than all the undertakers in the county combined, and the only thing he thought worth sweating over was his girlfriend of the month.

"I had some business to take care of across the street."

Russ resisted the urge to shift his gaze to the whitewashed-brick building that housed Jamie's office.

"What business do you have with Satan?"

J.D. scowled. "You know, if I was half as ticked off with Jamie as you are—"

"I'm not ticked off at Jamie. I don't like her. Under the circumstances, you shouldn't be dealing with her, either." Russ wasn't talking about his divorce, though family loyalty, with the exception of Robbie, should count for something. No, having won a damn fine settlement against one Calloway, Jamie was after another, representing J.D.'s wife, Laurie, in their split.

"I'm not dealing with her. That's why I waited until I knew she would be gone to come over this way."

Russ did look down at the building then. There were two good-sized windows, one in reception and one in the office. And through the first, he could see Lys Paxton sitting at her desk, using the computer. Her black hair concealed the buds that were usually plugged into her ears, but her head was bobbing, her entire body moving to music only she could hear.

He looked back at his cousin. "Lys Paxton? Give me a break."

His cousin bristled. "Lys and I used to date. There's nothing wrong with her."

"Yeah, right." She was young, more than a little freaky and didn't like Calloways. Plus she worked for Jamie and she'd once dated J.D. That was five strikes Russ could come up with in ten seconds.

"Besides, I haven't even talked to her today. Jamie hadn't left yet, so I came up here."

"Yeah, well, she's gone now."

"Watching her, were you?" J.D. asked with a smirk.

Russ pushed away from the window, returned to the door where he'd been working when his first interruption had come along and crouched, pry bar in hand. "You know, J.D., going out with your estranged wife's lawyer's paralegal might rank as one of the stupidest ideas you've ever come up with."

J.D. went to the window, no doubt watching Lys. "Knock it off, Russ. You're not my father, my brother, my lawyer, my priest or my boss. You don't get to tell me what to do."

"Someone needs to."

"Yeah, someone needs to set you straight, too, but I don't see you taking advice from anyone."

Russ scowled hard, focusing his irritation inward so he didn't inadvertently damage the piece of trim he was removing. "My life is fine."

"Yeah, you've got your work, your work and, oh, yeah, your work."

"Yeah, well, I don't have Jamie Munroe after my ass."

"Anymore. At least I'm smart enough to hire Robbie."

The pry bar slipped, leaving a mark in the plaster as well as the back of Russ's hand. He swore silently. "Dracula has gone out, and the bloodsucker-in-training is alone in their lair. You wanna make life harder for yourself, go ahead. Have at it. Just get the hell out of here and let me work."

J.D.'s smile was tight and hard, bearing an eerie resemblance to the only enduring memory Russ had of his father, who'd died when he was seven. "Yeah, well, like I said, you've got your work."

Russ listened until his footsteps were drowned out by the other workers in the house, then heaved a deep breath. Damn straight, he had his work.

And it was all he wanted.

The office of the psychologist Jamie had come to Augusta to see was located in a small enclave of similar offices near the Medical College of Georgia. She'd spent two hours listening to him assure her beyond a shadow of a doubt that her client had suffered egregiously at the hands of her husband. Now what she needed was an expert witness for her expert witness, because she was pretty convinced that Laurie and the doctor had cooked up a scheme to wring big bucks out of J. D. Stinson.

"He's a Calloway, you know," the doctor had mentioned near the end of the conversation.

What the hell did that mean? Jamie wondered as she unlocked her car with the remote, then opened the door to let the heat escape. Were all Calloway men genetically inclined to dole out abuse to their wives? Did all Calloways share some sense of entitlement that made them above the law? Were all Calloways rich enough to pay off disgruntled ex-wives whether the wives deserved payment?

She set her bag on the passenger seat, then peeled off her sweater. The doctor's office had been cold; the warm leather felt wonderful against her skin. Once the chill had seeped away, she stuck the key in the ignition and turned and…nothing. Another try, another nonresponse.

Grabbing her cell phone, she climbed out again and walked to the nearest shade under a lace-canopied tree. She knew nothing about mechanical things; popping the trunk told her as much about the engine as popping the hood did. So she did what she usually did when she was stuck: she called Lys. Within thirty sweltering minutes, a tow truck arrived to transport her car to the garage and soon after that, a car rental agency delivered a replacement. Jamie gratefully signed the paperwork, then slid inside, where the air conditioner was blasting on frigid.

Deciding to forego dinner alone, she headed back to Copper Lake. It was a lovely drive, quick on the interstate, peaceful on the two-lane state road. She'd never heard of the town until she'd met Russ and Robbie in law school and had visited only three weekends with Russ before he got married. Still, when she'd been looking for someplace to run away to after life had gone to hell in Macon and Robbie had suggested Copper Lake, it had seemed *right.* Immediately she'd felt as if she belonged. She'd borrowed office space from Robbie until she'd had enough clients to justify her own place, and she'd bought a house, made a few friends—and a few enemies, but at least they weren't the type to try to kill her.

She hoped.

Robbie was worried that her mystery man might be just that type. She hoped he was being overly protective. Everything the guy had done so far had been innocent. A vase of gorgeous flowers. A box of to-die-for chocolate liqueur candies. A scrawled note after a verdict that read *Congratulations. The best lawyer won.*

Innocent. Even if there was something inherently creepy about it. Even if it did rouse old memories, old discomforts.

It was after six-thirty when she drove into Copper Lake. She went downtown and turned at the east corner of the square to pull into a space right in front of her office. She would want to make notes on the interview with Dr. Sleaze, she'd told Lys. It wouldn't take long, then she could head home for dinner alone in front of the TV.

One thing she couldn't blame her admirer for: she didn't like being alone in the building. She'd been alone in the office in Macon when her former client's father had paid a visit. She'd forced herself to deal with the fear that night had created—not conquer it, but cope with it. She made herself come in here once every week or two, even when the work, like tonight, could be done just as easily at home. She forced herself to be brave, or at least pretend.

Everything was quiet. She locked the entrance behind her, then locked the reception door. Lys always left a few lamps burning, and they were on now, lighting her way into her office. The blinds were drawn, per Lys's routine. No need to advertise that Jamie was there.

As if the car parked out front wasn't advertisement enough.

Jamie got comfortable at the computer, aware of the window behind her, opened a document file and began typing. She didn't like the idea of calling Laurie Stinson's psychologist to testify. She found the guy a little too smug, too condemning of J.D. and his family when he'd never met any of them. Just like everyone else, there were good Calloways and bad ones. Not wanting to be married to Laurie anymore didn't automatically make J.D. one of the bad ones.

Outside a car door thudded, stilling Jamie's fingers on the keyboard. She wasn't the only one downtown tonight, she reminded herself. The restaurant on the other side of the square was open until eight, the coffee shop until nine. Sophy Marchand, who owned the quilt store next door, lived upstairs; the street was the only place for her and her visitors to park.

Still, Jamie typed faster, leaving the typos to fix later. As soon as she finished, she saved the file, shut off the computer and, with a rush of relief, headed for the door.

The outer hallway was exactly the way she'd left it—lights on, stairs empty, door locked. She paused in the foyer to locate the keys for the rental, and movement outside caught her attention. A man crouched beside her car, next to the driver's door, and he was fiddling with something.

Her first impulse was to run into the bathroom in her office, locking every door behind her, and call for help. Her second was to take a deep breath. The street was well-lit, and there were people in the square. And this was Copper Lake, her office, her sidewalk. She was safe there.

She stepped outside as the man leaned closer to the car. The door swung shut with a soft whoosh, and she quietly turned the key in the lock before taking a step toward him. "Can I help you with something?"

He stiffened, and the air between them practically shimmered. The tightness in her gut warned her it was Russ before he glanced over his shoulder, but it didn't lessen the impact of coming face-to-face with him for the first time in months. It didn't make the derision in his blue eyes any easier to take.

Slowly he stood, and she watched. His jeans, cleaner than what he'd worn earlier, fitted just as snugly, and his T-shirt looked a luscious size too small. With his impressive muscles flexing, his dark hair cut really short and his jaw stubbled with beard, he looked too damn sexy for her own good.

"Sorry," he said in a tone that clearly said he wasn't. "I didn't hear the portals opening."

The portals of hell. She'd heard some of the names he called her—bloodsucker, Satan, queen of the dark. She would have been amused by them, maybe even proud of them, if they'd come from someone else.

"What are you doing to my car?"

His gaze dropped to the object in his hands. He turned it over a time or two, then held it out. "This was wedged behind the tire. I pulled it out."

When she didn't reach for it, he laid it on the hood of the car. It was a thin piece of wood, maybe six inches long, with nails hammered through, their points extending several inches on the other side.

"Is that one of those strips used to hold carpet in place?"

"Not with 20d nails. It must have fallen out of the Dumpster when they emptied it this afternoon."

"Yeah, and the wind just blew it behind my tire." And backing out over it would have surely flattened the tire.

Apparently the same thought occurred to him. His scowl deepened and turned about ten degrees colder. "If I wanted your tire flat, there are quicker ways to do it that don't leave evidence behind. Like this." He slipped a knife from his pocket and unfolded the blade with ease, then twirled it between his fingers.

Blood rushed, echoing in her ears, and for a moment, just a moment, her chest grew too tight to allow any but the smallest of breaths. She took a step back, then forced herself to hold her ground, to breathe, to swallow the knot of fear in her throat, as she struggled to concentrate on his words.

"I didn't even know this was your car, and I don't give a damn whether you get a flat."

Her gaze locked on his face. He wasn't someone to fear. He might hate her, but he wouldn't hurt her. And she had no doubt he was being truthful. He had no interest whatsoever in her, beyond the fact that her existence annoyed him.

But the wood hadn't just magically appeared underneath her car, wedged, as he'd said, against the tire. It hadn't been there when she parked, or the tire would have already lost its air.

Maybe the mystery guy had left it. Better yet, maybe someone walking along the street had kicked it. Maybe a passing vehicle had caught the edge of it and sent it spinning, or some juvenile delinquent had put it there deliberately.

"You always look under neighboring cars before you get in your own?" she asked, edging forward enough to pick up the wood without getting close to him.

His mouth flattened, and one side quirked downward. "I opened the passenger door to get a flashlight and some papers fell out."

She could believe that. In law school, she'd never gone anywhere with him that he hadn't had to clear papers, books and other detritus to make room for her.

"I should thank you, I suppose, for not leaving it there to ruin the tire."

His mouth thinned even more. "Like I said,

I didn't know it was your car." Closing the knife with a snap, he returned it to his pocket, took a heavy-duty flashlight from the bed of the truck and started across the street.

She watched until he disappeared into the shadows of a live oak before she unlocked the car door. She tossed her bag on the passenger seat and the wood strip in the floorboard, and was about to slide inside when a familiar car turned the corner.

Lys slowed to a stop behind her and rolled the passenger window down, looking from Jamie to the pickup truck beside her before frowning. "You see Prince Charmless?" she asked sourly.

"Yeah, I did. What are you doing out?"

"Picking up a pizza."

"You know, Luigi's delivers."

"Yeah, but this way I get to anticipate that first bite all the way home. Want to come over and share?"

Jamie shook her head. "It's been a long day. I just want to get home."

"You'll regret it when you're looking in your freezer at nothing but boxed dinners. I'll see you tomorrow."

"Yeah. Be careful."

"Always," Lys replied with a grin before driving away.

Jamie got into the car, started the engine on the first try and headed home. Her house was little more than a mile from downtown, in a neighborhood where the yards were big, the houses were old and the trees were older. The house was white siding above dusty red-brick, with the shutters painted black. The steps leading to the front door were brick, as well, and arched out from the foundation in half-round tiers, each anchored by pots of brightly blooming flowers.

She pulled into the driveway, stopping even with the sidewalk. She unlocked the gleaming black door, an elegant contrast to the brass kick plate, then braced herself before opening the door. Mischa, best friend, companion and confidant, rocketed into her with enough force to knock her against the jamb, then abruptly the dog dropped to her haunches, eyes wide, just the tip of her broad pink tongue showing. It was as close to a smile as a dog could get.

"Hey, sweetie, I've missed you, too. Do you know I turned down Luigi's Pizza just so I could come home and be with you?"

Mischa's ears perked at the magic word. She loved Jamie, pizza, an old red shoe and snuggling when she slept—not necessarily in that order.

"Don't you drool on my rug," Jamie admonished as she set her bag down at the foot of the stairs, then kicked off her shoes. "I said I turned down the *p-i-z-z-a*. We'll have to make do with what's in the kitchen."

Still looking hopeful, Mischa followed her down the hall and into the kitchen. A lone light burned above the sink, showing clean counters, gleaming pots hanging from a rack and a cooktop that looked as if it had come straight from the factory. Jamie wasn't much of a cook; the only appliance she used with any regularity was the microwave.

And Lys was right: she did regret turning down the pizza when she faced the stacks of frozen dinners in the freezer. Disappointed by her chicken-and-pasta choice, Mischa padded over to her food dish and munched on dry nuggets.

"Another exciting night," Jamie murmured as she punched the microwave buttons. "You and me alone."

Mischa looked at her, then went back to crunching.

Dull and alone were okay, Jamie reminded herself. She'd had excitement for a time, and it had almost killed her. She could handle dull and alone. She could even handle seeing Russ twice in one day.

Though, if that became the rule rather than the exception, it just might kill her, too.

Chapter 2

Predawn wasn't an unusual time for Russ to be out and about. He could get a good deal of work done before the crews or the office staff showed up. Getting up that early for Robbie, slumped in the passenger seat beside him, was apparently cruel and unusual punishment. His head tilted against the window, his eyes were closed and his snore was quiet. The guy could stay up until 5:00 a.m. partying, but ask him to get up then for a purpose, and he barely managed.

"Hey." Russ poked Robbie's shoulder as he

merged onto the Bobby Jones Expressway in Augusta. "We're almost there."

One eye opened. "Almost where?"

"The airport. Remember? The Keys? Fishing? Catching the big one?"

"I'll do that tomorrow. Need sleep."

"You can sleep on the plane."

"I could sleep right here if you'd shut up."

"Hey, I'm not the one who wanted the first flight out this morning. You should be damn grateful that I offered to drive you."

Robbie straightened in the seat, looking as if he was coming off the end of a three-day drunk. "I should have scheduled a noon flight."

"You lazy bum. You give the rest of us a bad name."

"With the old man gone, someone's gotta do it." Robbie rubbed his eyes, then combed his fingers through his hair. Once he got around the other passengers and the flight crew, especially if any of them were female and pretty, he would shake off his fatigue and act like the TV bunny, going and going. It was easy for him.

Not so for Russ. Oh, he had the energy. He just didn't like expending it on people.

Bush Field was coming to life as employees prepared for another start of business. Russ pulled to the curb near one of the entrances and faced his brother. "Have fun."

"I always do." Robbie opened the door and slid halfway out, then turned back. "Listen, if you don't mind…keep an eye on things, would you?"

He sounded serious—a rare enough occurrence in Russ's experience. "What things?"

"Just…things. If anything seems strange or wrong, tell Tommy about it."

Tommy Maricci's father had been a shift foreman in the Calloway logging operation for years, and Tommy, Russ and Robbie had raised a lot of hell before they'd all gone off to college. Now a detective with the Copper Lake police, Tommy was still raising hell with Robbie.

"What kind of things, Rob?" Russ asked again. "Are you in trouble?"

"No. But someone I know might be."

Someone he knew would include the whole damn town of Copper Lake. Narrowing down which one of them would take more energy and interest than Russ possessed.

Robbie got out, heaved his bags from the pickup bed, then grinned. "Give my best to Amanda Saturday."

Russ snorted. "I'll give *my* best to her. I don't want to get punched for mentioning your name. Have fun. Bring back some fish."

"Will do." Robbie slammed the door, picked up his bags and headed inside the terminal. Before he even reached the entrance, he'd fallen into step beside a pretty flight attendant and said something to make her flash a million-watt smile.

Grinning, Russ pulled into the lane and headed back toward the expressway and home. It was a long drive back to Copper Lake, the sun slowly rising on the horizon behind him, his schedule for the day playing through his mind. An inspection at the Forsythia Drive address, a problem with the tilers at the new clinic on the highway out of town, an appointment with the interior designer, the kitchen designer and the lighting designer at the condo project on the west side of the river, a stop by the accountant's office. If he was lucky, he might squeeze in an hour or two to work at River's Edge.

And if his luck ran the way it usually did, he'd run into Satan while he was there. At least he knew what car to look for this time. Idly he wondered if her car was in the garage and why she'd been working late last night. Whether he knew the person whose life she would be ruining next. How that piece of wood had gotten wedged behind her tire.

And the wind just blew it over, she'd said sarcastically. Not likely. Now that he took the time to consider it, neither was his theory that it had fallen from the Dumpster. The wood had been set securely behind the tire, nails up, a flat waiting to happen.

Was Jamie the friend of Robbie's who was in trouble? Understandable. Russ surely wasn't the first or last person she'd pissed off. But, knowing how he felt about her, would Robbie ask him, even in a roundabout way, to keep an eye on her?

Russ's grin was flat. Yeah. He would.

The road into Copper Lake took him past the turns for his mother's house, his grandparents' place, his own place. Granddad had given each of the grandchildren five acres—one thing Melinda hadn't been able to touch in the divorce. He had built a house there after she was gone, way back in the woods, damn near impossible to find. Old logging roads criss-crossed the hillsides, most of them leading nowhere. With the nearest house belonging to Rick and Amanda—a weekend place—and few visitors, Russ liked the isolation.

Once he reached town, he stopped at the

mom-and-pop doughnut shop for a cinnamon roll and a cup of coffee, then considered which project to check first. The house on Walton Way was closest—ninety years old, a complete remodel from inside out, nothing special or challenging about it.

Except that it was directly across the street from Jamie's house. He'd known that when he accepted the job and hadn't given a damn...but he also hadn't been over there before she left for work or after she'd likely be home for the day. Coincidence? Or subconscious decision?

He would like to say coincidence. He would like to believe it, too.

"Hey, Russ." Smelling of sweat and tobacco, Tommy Maricci slid into the chair opposite him. He wore shorts, a T-shirt and running shoes, and his skin was damp, his black hair sticking to his head. A pack of cigarettes showed in the breast pocket of the shirt, and his plate held two jelly doughnuts.

"You're the only person I know who jogs

across town to get doughnuts and has a smoke on the way," Russ commented.

"I'm down to five cigarettes a day. Don't screw with me."

"How's crime?"

"Booming. You take Robbie to the airport?"

"Yeah. If he wasn't snoring, he was bitching about the time." Russ thought again of Robbie's request as he washed down a chunk of roll with coffee. "Is there anything going on with him that I should know about? Is he in trouble?"

Tommy raised his brows. "Robbie? In trouble?"

Only since he was old enough to walk and follow Russ and Rick on their adventures. Their family name was the only thing that had kept the three of them out of the legal system when they were teenagers, and the courtesy had extended to Tommy on more than one occasion. Not that they'd been *bad*. Just high-spirited, their mom said.

"What about one of his friends? Someone,

maybe a female, who might drag him into her problems?"

Tommy shrugged. "You'd have to ask him about that. Or her. You have a particular female in mind?" After a moment, he grinned. "Of course you do. Only one woman still in town gives you that look."

Russ scowled. "Let her take half of every-thing *you* own, and see how warm and fuzzy she makes you feel."

"She didn't take it, man. Judge Whitley did."

"Based on the crap she let Melinda tell him."

"Come on. Everybody knows you didn't run around on Melinda, and everybody damn well knows you never mistreated her."

Not everyone, Russ thought, his muscles tightening until he felt a headache coming on. A lot of people had listened to Melinda's lies, and they'd assumed the worst of him. Clearly, the judge had believed them. Why else would he have rewarded Melinda so richly for being an unfaithful wife?

"Back to the subject," he said, knowing he sounded stiff and not caring. "Is Robbie involved in anything even remotely that could cause trouble for him?"

"He's a lawyer. He's friendly with everybody. He's a Calloway. Of course he could get into trouble. But that's nothing new."

If trouble doesn't find you, you go looking for it, their mother used to say. Was that after they'd gotten caught painting all the high-school windows in the school colors of blue and gold? Or maybe when Rick had gotten his nose broken in a fight after football practice and Russ and Robbie, despite being younger and smaller, had jumped in to help him. They'd held their own, too. Or the time they'd gotten caught racing for pink slips. Or…

"Why are you worried about him?" Tommy asked. "Did he say something?"

"Just to let you know if anything strange happened while he's gone."

Tommy considered it while he ate the last of

his doughnut, then shrugged again. "If he's got a problem and he hasn't talked about it with you or me, how serious can it be?"

Good point. Robbie wasn't the sort to keep things to himself. If he had a thought on something, and he always did, he shared it. He wasn't a secretive sort of guy.

Tommy wadded up his napkin, then stuffed it into the empty coffee cup. "If anything strange does happen, you know how to find me. Otherwise, I'll see you around."

"Yeah," Russ agreed absently. "I'll see you."

"How was your frozen dinner last night?"

Jamie looked up to find Lys standing in the doorway, a bag slung over her shoulder and two boxes in hand. One bore the green and red of the Krispy Kreme doughnut shop down the block; the other was from Luigi's Pizza, no doubt bearing leftovers from Lys's own dinner the night before.

"Very good. Grilled chicken, bowtie pasta

and fire-roasted veggies in a low-fat cream sauce. Yum."

"Uh-huh." Coming closer, Lys set both boxes on the desk, then pulled two cans of diet pop from her bag. "Sounds better than it tasted, I bet. Any word on your car?"

"I'm supposed to call the garage later today to get the bad news." Jamie opened the pizza box and lifted out a slice heavy with toppings. "I love cold pizza for breakfast."

"I know." Lys chose a glazed doughnut from the other box, holding it over a napkin, and settled into one of the two client chairs. Her slim sheath and three-inch heels were black and, with her sleek black hair and porcelain-delicate skin, should have looked stark, but it worked for her. It made Jamie, in khaki trousers and pale blue shirt, feel dumpy.

"How long were you here last night?" Lys asked.

"Not long. Half an hour, maybe."

"Any trouble?"

Immediately Russ popped into Jamie's mind. In anyone's book, he was trouble with a capital *T,* but not, she was pretty sure, what Lys was referring to.

"Anything new from your secret admirer?" Lys clarified.

After another bite of pizza, Jamie told her about the nail-studded wood.

As she'd feared, Lys looked concerned. "You think he wanted your tire to go flat so he could…play the white knight for you? Offer to change it? Give you a ride home? Jeez, Jamie…"

"It could have been an accident." She'd been telling herself that every time the incident came to mind, but she hadn't managed to convince herself yet. "It could have just been kids being brats."

"Or it could have been a setup to get you in this guy's debt—or into his car, alone some-where. Did you call the police?"

"No." It seemed so petty. After all, no

damage had been done, and the motive was purely speculation.

"Do you still have the wood?"

"It's in the car."

Lys laid down the doughnut and held out her hand. "Give me your keys. I'll put it in the vault for safekeeping. The police may want it later."

Jamie gave her the keys, then picked up the pizza again. Cold cheese, peppers, Canadian bacon and extra onions on a thin crust were particularly comforting this morning. She polished off that piece and made a good start on the next by the time Lys returned, wood strip in hand. She disappeared into the file room—an honest-to-God vault from the days when the building had housed a savings-and-loan—then returned to pick up her doughnut. "How did you find it?"

"I didn't. Russ did."

That made Lys sit straighter, alerting the way Mischa did to a squirrel intrusion. "Russ Calloway? He was poking around your car when this crap suddenly appeared?"

"Russ wouldn't have flattened my tire or changed it or offered me a ride home. He doesn't want my gratitude, and I'm the last person in the world he would play white knight for." Saying the words stirred an ache in Jamie's gut. There had been a time when they'd meant so much to each other, when she'd had such hopes for their future. Now he felt nothing but hostility for her. How had they come to this?

Well, for starters, representing his ex in their divorce hadn't been the best way to stay on good terms with him. But *someone* had had to take Melinda's case. The marriage was beyond saving, and Jamie had been new to town, looking for clients to build her practice. And Robbie had assured her it was okay. Russ was a lawyer himself. He would understand that it was just business.

Yeah, right.

"White knight, giving you a ride—those would have been secret admirer motives," Lys said. "Russ Calloway wouldn't have secret admirer motives."

Another twinge of pain. "And what kind of motives would he have?"

"Stalker motives. Vandalism. Harassment. Pure meanness. He doesn't like you, Jamie. He says horrible things about you. Maybe he wants to punish you. Maybe he wants to hurt you."

The pizza felt heavy and unwelcome in Jamie's stomach. She set the remains of the second slice down and took a cautious drink of pop, grateful when it stayed down. "Not Russ. He's a decent guy—"

"Who's mad as hell at you." Lys leaned forward, her dark eyes troubled. "Who happened to be right there when the wood showed up. Who has access to wood and nails on the job site. You said he found it and was removing it when you came out. What if he was really putting it there? He'd have no choice but to take it out again or be caught."

Jamie pictured the scene from the night

before in her mind—the dusky evening, the man crouched beside her car, his back to her. She hadn't even recognized him until an instant before he'd turned; she certainly hadn't seen exactly what he was doing. Had he been removing the wood strip...or wedging it in place?

Common sense waved its little fingers for her attention. For God's sake, this was Russ they were talking about. His feelings for her aside, he was a good guy, respected in business, adored by his family, admired by his crews. Hell, she'd *loved* him. He wasn't the type who would vandalize a woman's car, not even hers. He wouldn't harass her, would never hurt her.

"Not Russ," she said aloud, and she believed it. "Okay, so he's holding a grudge—"

"A grudge? It's been three years, and he still calls you Satan."

The pang was smaller this time, barely a discomfort. "A little displaced anger isn't uncommon in a nasty divorce. Melinda left town. I'm the only one left to hate."

"Oh, yeah, sure. Every person who gets divorced feels that way toward the opposing counsel. It's a wonder that any lawyer will even take on a divorce case these days, isn't it?"

Lys's sarcasm made Jamie smile a little. "You've noticed that I've cut way back on divorces, haven't you?" While she'd practiced criminal law in Macon, it was tough to special-ize in Copper Lake. Like the other lawyers in town, she did a little bit of everything, from criminal trials to estate planning to contract negotiation. While she would prefer to never handle another divorce, she still took on a few. It was part of practicing law in a small town.

"Jamie—"

"Lys, it was probably just kids who found the wood at the construction site and thought it'd be funny to flatten someone's tire. Until Russ showed up, my car was the only one on the block. I got picked by default."

Lys was reluctant to accept that version of events; it was clear in her grudging expression and tone. "You think so?"

"I do." And if she kept saying it, before long she would believe it. Not a stalker. Not a threat. Just kids, or really bad luck.

As the digital clock on the wall rolled over to 9:00 a.m., the phone began ringing, first the main line, then the rollover. Rising, Lys put both calls on hold, then gazed at Jamie a moment. "You be careful anyway."

The warmth of affection rushed through Jamie. Lys had been a good friend from the moment they'd met on Jamie's second full day in town. She'd applied for the job of paralegal and secretary, and had provided support, laughter and plenty of shoulders to lean on when Jamie needed them. She hoped she'd been as good a friend in return.

The morning was busy, but they still made time for their construction-watching break, though with more care this time. Jamie scanned all the vehicles parked along the streets, looking for the 1972 Chevrolet Cheyenne pickup that was Russ's baby—one piece of property Melinda had desperately wanted but failed to gain ownership of—and she studied every guy with dark hair, broad shoulders and a long, lean body. Ogling a site full of hard bodies to find one hard body in particular: nice work if you could get it, she thought wryly as she relaxed.

"Remember I said I need a date bad?" Lys murmured as she slid her feet back into her heels, then stood, about to return to work. "J.D. asked me out yesterday."

"J. D. Stinson? The Calloway cousin? Our client's soon-to-be ex-husband?"

"I didn't say yes." Lys gave her a chiding look. "I understand conflict of interest. But…we used to date. Before you came to town. For a while."

"What happened? Did you break his heart?"

Lys's smile was broad and extraordinarily

white against the crimson slash of her lipstick. "You've got to care about someone besides yourself before you can get your heart broken. We just lost interest. He met someone else, and so did I."

Lys hadn't been in a serious relationship in the three years Jamie had known her. She didn't ask how it had worked out with her someone else. The answer was pretty clear.

"He and Laurie have been separated six weeks, and he's already dating again?"

"He never *stopped* dating. A lot of what Laurie says may be bull, but the infidelity stuff—that's all true."

"So he's not too broken up by the divorce."

"Like I said, you have to care about someone besides yourself." With a wide-eyed shrug, Lys left the office for her own desk.

Jamie couldn't imagine it as she turned back to her desk and slid the computer keyboard closer. Marriage was a big deal. A person should go into it with hopes, dreams and commitment. Of course no one was guaranteed happily ever after, but if that wasn't your goal, if you weren't willing to work and compromise, why bother marrying at all?

If she ever got married, it would be with the intention of striving for the till-death-do-us-part. If divorce became inevitable, she would be heartbroken, but she would know she'd done everything possible to avoid it.

Like Russ. Even Melinda had admitted in an unguarded moment that none of it was his fault. He'd tried to work with her, had compromised and given in, had even been willing to go to marriage counseling. But all she'd wanted was out, with as many of their assets as she could get.

And Jamie had helped her get them. If she could somehow return to the past and undo her involvement in a particular case, that one would be at the top of the list.

Then she rubbed the spot low on her ribcage that still ached at times, though the wound was long since healed, and amended the thought: Russ's divorce would be second on the list.

She worked through the rest of the morning, hardly noticing the passage of time until her stomach growled. It was after one o'clock, and the satisfaction from morning pizza was long gone. Rising from her chair, she slung the strap of her purse over one shoulder and went into the outer office. "I'm hungry. Want to get a sandwich at the deli?"

Lys looked up from the fax machine she was feeding. "Sure. Why don't you go on over and order, and I'll be there as soon as I finish sending the Thompkins stuff to his new lawyer in Miami. I'll have a vegetarian wrap."

"With ranch dressing, baked veggie chips and bottled water."

Lys gave her a thumbs-up before turning back to the machine.

It was another warm day with only the thinnest of clouds in the sky. Humidity hung heavy, trapping the fragrance of the flowers that bordered the square close to the ground. Jamie loved the mix of smells: flowers, greenery, dampness, tasty aromas from Krispy Kreme, the coffee shop and the restaurants along the block. She fancied she could even catch a whiff of fresh-sawn lumber from the River's Edge project—which, she congratulated herself, she hadn't so much as glanced at since stepping outside.

Ellie's Deli occupied prime corner-of-the-square real estate, an old building that had begun life as a general store. Broad steps led to a porch, and a few items there harked back to its past: metal advertising signs mounted on the walls, a checkerboard balanced atop an old wooden barrel and rockers, silvered with age.

Jamie placed their order, took a number and went looking for a table in her favorite section, a long narrow enclosure that had once been a back porch. Screens had been replaced by windows that looked out on Ellie Chase's kitchen garden.

Her favorite table was empty. Setting down her bag, she slid into the chair and tension she'd hardly noticed eased away. It was a lovely place, with exposed brick walls and a well-worn brick floor, with all the glass and light and ceiling fans lazily stirring the air. The noise from the main dining room was muted, and the proximity to the kitchen allowed the fragrance of hot bread to seep into the space, along with hints of desserts baking.

She was so lost in *noticing* that she didn't realize she wasn't alone until a pair of boots came into view through the glass tabletop. Work boots, spattered with paint and mud. Faded jeans, also spattered. A snug-fitting T-shirt with a coat of chalky dust overlaying its crimson hue.

And a world-class scowl.

The muscles in her neck knotted and her jaw clamped together hard. This wasn't fair. No more surprise sightings. No more sightings at all if he was going to look at her as if she were something nasty in need of squishing.

Russ rested one hand on the back of her chair and bent closer. "I thought I saw blood oozing from the brick." Uninvited, he sat down in the chair to her left.

She forced a smile. "Watch it, or I might turn the sky dark, too."

Coincidentally, the sun disappeared behind a cloud, shadow falling over the garden. She resisted the urge to laugh at the timing. He clearly felt no such urge.

"Have you dragged my brother into something he can't handle?"

Jamie kept her gaze even, unflinching. Russ didn't even make the list of people Robbie might have discussed her admirer-stalker with. He and Jamie occupied distinctly separate areas of Robbie's life. If he'd tattled to anyone, it would have been Tommy Maricci or his cop brothers.

"Offhand, I can't think of anything Robbie can't handle." Then she slyly asked, "We are talking about Robbie, aren't we? You're not accusing me of impropriety with Rick or Mitch, are you?"

His response was a snort, but it said enough. His older brothers wouldn't be interested. She wasn't pretty enough, sexy enough, to tempt them away from their wives, but no woman was. Fidelity might not have meant much to all Calloways—J. D. Stinson came to mind—but it was important to these four brothers.

And Melinda had taken such pleasure in publicly airing all the dirty details of her extramarital affairs. A broken heart, wounded pride and a bruised ego—Russ had hit the trifecta.

"What's going on?" His voice was deep, tautly controlled, a lot like Robbie's, except she could count the number of times she'd heard anger in Robbie's voice on one hand. It was all she'd heard from Russ for three years.

"Maybe you should ask him."

"I did. All he would say was that someone he knows is in trouble."

"And you automatically assume it's me?"

"Who else is as deserving?"

Her first inclination was to ignore the tiny ache in her chest. As her number was called over the intercom, she decided to go with her second. Rising, she put one hand on the back of his chair, leaned close enough to smell sunshine, sweat and dust and softly said, "Bite me, Russ."

She made it halfway to the hall that led to the main dining room before he caught up with her. "If something's going on, leave Robbie the hell out of it."

She didn't slow her pace. "Robbie's a big boy. He can make decisions for himself."

"I'm not kidding."

She gave the girl behind the counter a tight smile as she claimed the trays that held her and Lys's lunches, then faced him again. "Give it up, Russ. I've been threatened by people way scarier than you. If you have enough energy to worry about someone's life, make it your own.

You're way more screwed up than Robbie will ever be."

"You don't know what the hell—"

The bell over the door dinged, announcing a new arrival. Russ looked that way, and so did Jamie. Lys's gaze locked on them, and she charged forward like an overprotective bulldog in puppy's clothing.

Jamie shoved Lys's tray into her hands, then bared her teeth at Russ in a parody of a smile. "It's been fun talking to you. What do you say we wait another three years to do it again?"

Color stained his dark skin crimson, and his gaze turned stormy. She didn't wait to hear what he might say, but took Lys's arm and steered her toward the back. It wasn't until they'd turned the corner into the glassed-in porch that Lys spoke.

"Good show. Now would you please let go of my arm so the blood can start flowing again?"

Contritely Jamie did so. "I'm sorry. It's just…"

"I know. It's just Russ."

He'd been the reason for a lot of emotions in her life—happiness, giddiness, need, desire, lust, satisfaction, affection, love, anger, betrayal, headache, heartache and every other kind of ache. He'd been the best part of her life for a time, and the worst.

One of these days, he wasn't going to be any part. She promised herself that.

Just as soon as she figured out how to perform magic.

Chapter 3

In less than a day and a half, three people had offered criticism of Russ's life. He hadn't asked for advice, hadn't given a clue that he was open to suggestions, so why the hell couldn't they keep their opinions to themselves?

And after three years of pretty decent avoidance, why the hell did he have to keep running into Jamie?

"Because God doesn't like you," he muttered as he walked into the kitchen.

It was after eight o'clock. The sun had set,

darkness had settled in, and he was still on the job. The day had turned into the day from hell—too many appointments, too much work, too little time—and his run-in with Jamie at lunch had only made it worse. He'd walked out of the deli with a pounding headache, and the aspirin tablets he'd taken were eating a hole in his stomach. He should have gotten something to eat before the last dose, but anything he ate right now would just aggravate the burning in his gut.

But this Walton Way job was his last stop, and then he was heading home. A night's sleep would make everything better—and no matter what else was going on in his life, he always slept like a baby. He was lucky that way.

The work on this remodel was slow going. The house was old, and they kept running into unforeseen problems, like wiring that wasn't up to code and pipes that had to be replaced. Another few weeks, and he could scratch this one off his list.

Another few weeks, and he wouldn't have to

come back into Jamie's neighborhood until someone else hired him.

He shouldn't have spoken to her at the deli. He should have just walked past as if she were a total stranger. She was right: Robbie *was* grown. He didn't always make the smartest decisions—his continued friendship with Jamie proved that—but he was old enough to face the consequences.

The next time Russ saw her, he *would* ignore her. He didn't want anything to do with her; she didn't want anything to do with him. Simple solution. They would act like strangers, and before long they would really be strangers.

He finished his walk-through of the house, then let himself out the front door, yawning as he locked the deadbolt. The homeowners were staying with the husband's parents during the remodel, and the wife called every other day wanting to know when she could move home again. Russ, his secretary, his subs and everyone on his crew who'd had to deal with the woman would be as happy when that day came as she would be.

He was walking to his truck in the driveway when a familiar voice across the street caught his attention. "Mischa? Mi-i-i-scha."

The call was distant, coming from the back of Jamie's house. A sissy name for a pet. Probably a sissy cat.

Jamie's outside lights came on, then the front door opened. He refused to let his gaze linger; the instant she stepped outside, he focused narrowly on unlocking his pickup, on opening the door and tossing the clipboard he carried into the passenger seat. He was about to slide behind the wheel when her voice sounded again, this time only slightly calmer than a scream.

"Mischa! Oh my God!"

He couldn't stop himself from looking, even if it was just a damn cat. The lights on either side of her door shone down on a large form, and Jamie, damn near prostrate over it. Had she fallen? Was she hurt?

None of his business. If she had a problem, let her call someone for help. She had friends besides Robbie—freaky Lys Paxton, for starters—and the police were duty bound to come if she called. His head hurt. His stomach hurt. He'd dealt with enough for one day. He was going home.

But when he moved, it wasn't to step up into the truck. Swearing with every step, he stalked down the driveway, across the deserted street and into her yard. As he drew closer, he could see that the form was a dog, huge, black and tan, lying motionless on the top step. Shivers rippled through Jamie, and her words were frantic.

"It's okay, Mischa, you're okay, baby. Wake up. Come on now, open your eyes. You can't be…Mischa, you can't…"

Tears. Jamie Munroe was crying. He wouldn't have thought her capable of it.

He took the steps two at a time and crouched

beside the dog. It could have been asleep, except no one could sleep through the shaking Jamie was giving it. "What happened?"

She looked up, startled, and swiped at her tears with one hand. "I don't know. I let her out a few minutes ago, like I do every night, and she didn't come back."

The dog was breathing, slow and easy. Running his hands over its body, at least on the side he had access to, didn't reveal any signs of obvious injury, but when he lifted its head, something crackled beneath his fingers. Heavyweight paper, index card-size, tied to the dog's collar with a ribbon.

He worked it out from beneath the dog, read the message neatly printed on it, then lifted his gaze to Jamie. "What the hell…?"

I can get to you as easily as I got to Mischa.

She stared at the words as if they made no sense, then a great shudder jerked her gaze back to the dog. "Oh my God, Mischa…"

Russ ripped off the note and slid it into his

hip pocket. "Get your car keys. We've got to get him to the vet."

She scrambled to her feet and disappeared into the house, returning seconds later with her keys and purse. While she unlocked the car and opened the rear door, he heaved ninety pounds of limp animal into his arms, gritting his teeth with the effort. Getting the dog into the backseat of the rental wasn't any easier. It took both of them, supporting, tugging and pushing, and he was out of breath by the time they were done.

He held out his hand, and she slapped the keys into his palm, then wiggled into the back with the dog. He adjusted the seat for his legs, backed out of the long drive and headed out of the neighborhood. Sliding his cell phone from the clip on his belt, he offered it to her. "Call Yancy and tell him we're on our way. His number's in the phone book."

What the hell was he doing getting involved with this? He didn't like animals. Didn't like

Jamie. Didn't care what had happened to the dog or who had left that note on its collar or whether Jamie was in danger. With Robbie out of the state for the time being, he didn't give a damn about anything.

But there was no way she could move the dog on her own, and his mother, Rick, Mitch— all of them would have kicked his ass if he'd gone on home and left her there to deal with it. A Calloway—at least, their particular branch of the family—didn't walk away from someone in need, regardless of his opinion of her.

Yancy Yates's vet clinic was on the east side of town, a large cinder block building dating back to the 1920s. He was married to Russ's aunt Diane and lived in the rambling farm-house next door.

Yancy had already unlocked the door and turned on the lights. Looking surprised to see Russ, he helped him unload the dog and place it on a stretcher, then together they carried it into the back room of the clinic. Yancy checked the dog's breathing, listened to its heart and examined it thoroughly, keeping up a quiet murmur to Mischa, still out, and to himself.

"I'll draw some blood and send it to the lab," he said at last, "but my best guess is that she's been drugged."

Jamie's color was ashen under the florescent lights, and her voice was little more than a whisper. "With what?"

"I'll have to see the tox screen to know for sure. It could be something as simple as a sleeping pill or a sedative." Yancy looked from her to Russ and back again. "Why would anyone want to drug Mischa? I thought Russ here was your only enemy in town, and he would never harm an animal."

Russ's face warmed. Jeez, did everyone in Copper Lake know how much he resented Jamie? It wasn't as if he advertised the fact. Until lately, he hardly ever saw her, and other than a few outbursts three years ago, he never talked about her with anyone outside of a small group of friends and relatives.

Who apparently talked to everyone else.

Jamie didn't seem to notice the comment about him. "I don't know," she murmured, clearly not intending to mention the note. When she bent to stroke the dog's fur, Mischa breathed heavily, then rested her big head against Jamie's neck, as if seeking familiar comfort.

"Have you called the police?" Yancy asked.

"I didn't think about it."

"You should. Anyone who would drug someone's pet is obviously up to no good." Yancy rubbed one weathered hand over the dog's spine. "All we can do now is watch her. Odds are she'll get a good night's sleep, nothing else. I'll keep her here, and we'll have the results of the tox screen by noon tomorrow. Russ, you want to help me put her in that kennel over there?"

After they settled Mischa in the kennel,

Jamie knelt beside it, stroking the dog, whispering to her. She didn't look so much like Satan at that moment.

Finally, she got to her feet. "Thanks, Dr. Yates. You'll call me?"

"I've got your numbers. I'll keep you updated."

They left Yancy there, making notes on a chart, and walked outside into the muggy night. Still looking pale, Jamie waited in silence for him to unlock the car doors, but instead he faced her over the roof of the car.

"What the hell is going on?"

In the past thirty minutes, Jamie had gone from pleasantly tired to exhausted. Her jaw hurt, her nerves were on edge, and the last thing she wanted to do was talk. She just wanted to curl up someplace safe. But where was safe? Not her house. Not after what had happened to Mischa right outside her door.

What kind of lowlife would threaten her dog? Mischa wouldn't hurt a fly, though she might chase it around the room a few times. She wasn't a guard dog, would never attack. If someone broke into the house, she would hide under the bed, eyes closed and whimpering. She loved everyone.

But apparently not everyone loved her.

The bulk of the lights went off inside the clinic, throwing them into shadow. She gestured impatiently toward the car door and Russ unlocked it. She slid into the seat and fastened the seat belt, but she didn't kid herself that she'd escaped his questions. She couldn't be that lucky.

The first thing she smelled inside the car was the earthy fragrance Mischa always wore when she'd been outside. The instant Russ slid into the driver's seat, it was replaced by *his* scents—sweat, hard work, a faint hint of cologne, *him*. Familiar smells. Comforting.

Even though Russ Calloway was the last person on earth she could take comfort from.

Through the plate-glass window, she caught

a glimpse of Dr. Yates, still in the back room, no doubt checking on the other animals spending the night in his care. He was a good vet. Mischa would be safe with him.

Russ started the engine, powerful enough, but it had nothing on his own growl. "Well?"

"Someone wanted me to know that Mischa's vulnerable."

"No, someone wanted you to know that *you're* vulnerable. Someone who knows where you live, who knows your dog's name. Who?"

"I don't know."

"Oh, come on."

"I don't! If I did, I'd have his ass hauled off to jail for messing with Mischa." Threatening her was one thing. Threatening her dog… That was cold.

"What else has happened?"

She stared out the side window, hardly noticing the buildings they passed. "He's sent me flowers. Candy. A note."

Russ snorted. "Yeah, I saw the note."

The reminder of the message attached to Mischa's collar sent a shiver down her spine, and she hugged herself to contain it. "Another note. Congratulating me on a case."

"Why haven't you called the police?"

"I didn't think it was necessary." Couldn't *admit* it was necessary. Not again.

Hearing a rustle of movement, she glanced his way as he retrieved his cell and flipped it open. Feeling fairly certain he was looking up Tommy Maricci's number, she closed her eyes and rested her head against the seat.

Russ's conversation with Tommy was short. He shut the phone and set it in the cup holder. "Tommy's going to meet us at your house." He didn't look at her but kept his gaze locked on the road ahead. Both hands were on the wheel, and the muscles in his jaw were taut. He radiated tension.

But she was still glad to have him there. How would she have gotten Mischa to the vet's by herself? How would she have held herself together alone?

"Robbie knows about this."

It wasn't a question, but she answered anyway. "Yes."

"So you *are* the one dragging him into trouble."

There was no reason to feel guilty. She hadn't lied to him at the deli. She simply hadn't answered him at all, and that was her right. It wasn't as if they were friends, as if he had a stake in anything happening in her life. "I told him about it, but I didn't 'drag' him into anything. We just talked."

"And what did he think?"

"He said I should call the police. He thought it was weird."

He signaled for the turn off River Road onto her street. "What idiot wouldn't think it was weird?"

"I just hoped…" She'd convinced herself it was harmless weird. She'd fought too hard to get back a normal life; she hadn't wanted to surrender it without concrete evidence. She had that now.

The neighborhood was quiet as they drove through. She'd loved the area since the first time she'd seen it—the huge lots, the old charm of the houses, the trees, the privacy and the sense of *home*. In the two and a half years she'd lived there, she'd always looked forward to coming home. She'd always felt welcomed.

Until tonight.

Russ's truck was still parked in the Petrovskis' driveway, five hundred feet from her front door. How loudly had she shrieked when she'd found Mischa unresponsive on the steps?

Loudly enough to get his attention. To appeal to the decency that was inside him under all that hostility, to bring him to Mischa's aid. If he stayed angry with her for the rest of their lives, she would always be grateful for that.

He parked in her usual spot and shut off the

engine. She got out and, still close to the security of the car, looked around. Neither of the houses to the side could be seen from her vantage point; tall hedges of azaleas and red-tip shrubs hid them. The Petrovski house across the street had a few dim lights burning, and lights were on at their closest neighbor's, but much of the yards were in shadow.

Was he out there somewhere, watching? He'd come close to her house to reach Mischa; the dog never left the yard when she made her postdinner trips outside. Jamie had been inside, the television on, the dryer running, a book open on the arm of her favorite chair, blissfully unaware that someone had invaded her property. How easily could he have gained access to the house? She wouldn't have given a second thought to a noise at the back door; she would have assumed it was Mischa, unlocked the door and opened it without looking to let the dog in.

She shuddered.

Russ circled the car and started along the sidewalk toward the steps. The more distance he put between them, the more vulnerable she felt. Exactly what the mystery man wanted.

She caught up within a few steps, took the keys he offered and unlocked the door, but she hesitated at going inside. What if the stalker was in there, waiting for her?

Then he'd be disappointed to find Russ with her—and Tommy Maricci, who was turning into the driveway, followed by two officers in a marked car. Her comfort level eased up a notch or two.

"Any way this nutcase could have gotten inside the house?" Tommy asked as a greeting.

Jamie glanced down the long hallway. From the doorway, everything appeared as she'd left it, but that didn't mean anything. Had she locked the back door after futilely calling Mischa? Was the lock sturdy enough to keep him out? Had he broken a window somewhere in the shadows?

Her silence was answer enough. Tommy directed one of the men to check outside the house, the other to search inside. As soon as they went off in opposite directions, he gestured toward the door. "Let's go in the living room and talk."

It was harder stepping through the door than Jamie had expected. Damn it, she wouldn't let some pervert rob her of the comfort of her home. Squaring her shoulders, she walked into the hallway, then turned into the living room on the right.

Tommy didn't waste any time as he settled in an armchair. "I called Robbie on the way over here. He told me about the other incidents." A pause for effect. "He also told me about what happened in Macon. Is this a garden-variety stalker or could there be a connection?"

Russ, looking at the photographs on the fireplace mantel, turned around. "What happened in Macon?"

She'd decided to stand, but just the sharp

edge of his gaze made her rethink and sink onto the sofa at the nearest end. "If there's a connection, I can't see it. Shan Davis and his father are in prison. His mother left town before Shan's trial even started. There were no brothers or sisters, no relatives who came to the trial or visited him in jail."

Russ moved forward, no more than a foot or so, but the distance between them seemed to shrink immeasurably. She could feel the annoyance radiating from him. "Trial for what? In prison for what?"

Tommy was quiet, leaving her to answer. In a monotone, she did. "Nearly four years ago, I defended Shan Davis on murder charges. He'd confessed, then recanted, but there were witnesses, fingerprints, DNA. The best I was hoping for was a life sentence, but he received the death penalty. He was nineteen, an only child. His mother accepted that he was guilty and left town. His father never accepted it. He blamed me for the verdict, and he came to my office one night when I was working late. Fortunately, I'd ordered out for pizza, and the delivery guy scared him away."

Russ stared at her, his blue gaze so intent that she felt it, hot and damn near vibrating along her skin. "He didn't go to prison for visiting you at your office."

"No," she agreed. "He went to prison for stabbing me four times. Obviously, none of the wounds were fatal." Painful, yes, and terrifying. She'd been utterly certain she was going to die, and she hadn't been prepared. She'd prayed harder that night than ever before.

Who'd known prayers could be answered in the form of a Domino's delivery guy?

Russ's entire body stiffened, and his expression shifted from annoyance to anger. Was he regretting that Harlan Davis hadn't succeeded at killing her? Then someone else could have represented Melinda. Someone else could have been on the receiving end of his hostility for the past three years.

He opened his mouth, but before he gave voice to any words, Tommy spoke. "Why the hell didn't we hear anything about this?"

"I guess it wasn't big news outside of Macon." Actually, the story had been picked up by the media outside the city—one of those little filler pieces that took a few seconds' airtime or an inch or so of column space, heard or read and forgotten immediately.

"Robbie knew."

Jamie smiled faintly. There was an accusing undertone to Tommy's voice, like a child left out of the secret his friends shared. "So did Lys. I asked them not to tell anyone."

Robbie had been in Atlanta the night it happened; he'd gone straight to Macon from there, or he surely would have told someone in his family first. She'd been a mess—weak, in pain, terrified and filled with self-recriminations. She shouldn't have worked late at the office, shouldn't have dismissed Harlan Davis as just another angry parent, shouldn't have taken his son's case to begin with. She should have fought harder, should have been stronger both before and after, should have resisted being such a victim. She'd been ashamed of herself and hadn't wanted anyone to know.

Hadn't wanted Russ to know. He'd been married, after all, and happily, as far as she knew. He'd long since stopped caring about her.

"So that was why you came to Copper Lake. To feel safer."

"To make a new start." Then she shrugged. "And to feel safer."

"If this guy was part of that," Russ said, drawing her gaze to him, "why send the flowers and the candy? Why make it look like he's interested?"

"To throw us off," Tommy replied. "If we're looking for a wannabe boyfriend, we're not gonna be looking at the guy who tried to kill her. Are those the flowers?"

She nodded. The vase sat on the coffee table that separated sofa and chairs. A bit of the bloom was off the roses, their color not quite so vivid, their petals not quite so fresh.

"No tag, no card, no delivery info?"

"No. And there's nothing special about the vase. I have three or four just like it under the kitchen sink."

"But there was a card tonight."

Russ pulled the note from his pocket, dangling it by the ribbon, as one of the officers came into the room. Tommy directed him to bag the note. "You'll find Russ's fingerprints all over it," he said with good-natured sarcasm.

"There's something else at the office," Jamie said, then told him about the wood strip. "I can get it for you tonight or in the morning. And you'll find Russ's, Lys's and my fingerprints all over *it*."

"If we get you amateurs out of the way, we might have a chance at ID'ing this guy," Tommy grumbled. "I'll pick it up in the morning. In the meantime, you're not gonna stay here for the next few days, are you?"

Her chest tightened. Part of her wanted to. This was her home, her sanctuary. But the mere thought of the men leaving, of being there alone, of locking the doors and turning off the lights and knowing that she wasn't safe, was enough to make her knees weak.

"You can move in with Lys, can't you?" Tommy suggested.

"No. If I've got some psycho after me, there's no way I'm going near any of my friends' houses. I won't put them at risk. I can go to a motel." It wasn't a great choice. Once she checked in, she would still be alone. Would still be afraid.

Then, in a day filled with surprises, she got another.

Russ folded his arms across his chest, looking as distant and cold as ever and, in a hard voice, said, "You can stay with me."

It wasn't the worst idea Russ had ever had. That was marrying Melinda. But it wasn't the most sane, either, judging by the looks Jamie and Tommy were giving him. He shrugged off their surprise. "We're not friends, and I can take care of myself."

There was that protective streak his mother had instilled in him and his brothers. He didn't like the idea of any bastard menacing a woman, not even Jamie, and damned if he would stand by and do nothing. It wasn't a big deal. His house was difficult to find, and the bedrooms were at opposite ends. He usually left before sunrise and got back long after sunset. And the last six months of his marriage had proven that he could share a house with a woman without crossing paths with her.

"Okay," Tommy said at last. "Get what you need, Jamie. We'll wait."

Russ expected her to argue, to insist on doing things her way. She looked as if she wanted to, but in the end, she just nodded, then went upstairs.

"You know, if she disappears out there,

you'll be our prime suspect." Tommy was grinning. He damn well knew that Russ wasn't a danger to Jamie and was amused by it. "Man, Robbie's right. You *are* freakin' irrational where she's concerned."

Russ's only response was to leave the room and wait impatiently just outside the front door. That didn't stop Tommy from joining him. This time, though, he was dead serious.

"Don't make the mistake she did of thinking this is no big deal," he said quietly. "A nutcase who hurts animals will have no problem hurting people, especially the guy who gets between him and the woman he's obsessing over. Don't confuse isolation with security, and keep a weapon handy just in case. Stalkers don't always kill, but a lot of the time they do. Don't get caught unprepared."

Russ held his gaze, long and steady, for a time before nodding. He wasn't just offering Jamie a bed. He was offering to do exactly what Tommy had said: get between her and whoever was after her. It was one hell of a responsibility, but he didn't back down.

"Leave her car here," Tommy continued. "I don't want her driving those logging roads by herself. Too many places for an ambush. And she shouldn't tell anyone where she's staying, not even Lys. Anyone has to get hold of her outside the office, they can call her cell phone. Keep your eyes open, and if anything at all looks or even feels wrong, call 911 and tell them to call me."

Russ nodded again, then dug his keys from his pocket. "I'll get my truck."

If he'd left the Petrovski house five minutes earlier, he would have been home by now, would have eaten dinner and been kicked back in front of the television or the computer. Jamie and her overgrown dog wouldn't have been his problem. She would be going to a motel, where she would spend the night alone, worrying about her dog, worrying about her stalker and whether he'd followed her and, if not, how hard it would be for him to find her.

And remembering what had happened when her client's father had found her.

Moving stiffly, he unlocked the truck's passenger door and transferred the papers, files and mail from the seat into a box kept behind it just for that purpose, then brushed dried clumps of drywall mud from the seat out the open door. After circling the truck, he slid behind the wheel, started the engine, backed out of the long driveway and pulled into Jamie's drive as she came out of the house.

Tommy took a suitcase and garment bag, leaving her to carry a laptop case and another small bag. Russ watched them approach, Jamie listening earnestly to what Tommy had to say, stress bracketing her mouth, giving her a jittery look. Russ had never seen much real fear, but he recognized it now. That was why she was going with him without protest. Better to stay with her enemy than to face her fear alone.

Tommy hefted her bags into the truck bed while she climbed into the seat. Instantly Russ caught a whiff of perfume, something light, more exotic than sweet. It was the same fragrance she'd worn back in law school. His sheets had smelled of it, his clothes, but he couldn't recall the name of it. Couldn't say that he'd ever paid enough attention to know.

After rolling down the passenger window, Tommy closed the door, then fixed his gaze on each of them in turn. "This isn't a game, okay? You both take it seriously. Damned if I'm gonna tell Robbie something happened to either of you while he was gone."

Russ was feeling pretty damn serious. Jamie looked it, too, in spite of her shaky smile. "He would be unbearable, wouldn't he?"

"You know it. I'll come by your office in the morning."

"I'll be there."

Tommy stepped back with a grim nod, and Russ backed out of the driveway into the street.

Jamie fastened her seat belt, crossed her legs and folded her hands in her lap. Her expression, illuminated by the streetlights they passed, was grim, her jaw taut. As he turned north, she finally spoke. "I appreciate this."

His impulse was to respond flippantly, but he gestured in dismissal instead. He was sure she did appreciate his offer. She might not have taken the stalker seriously to start—though who could blame her for preferring flattery over fear? But she was a smart woman. Now that she knew the bastard was worthy of fear, she wouldn't take any stupid chances.

A smart woman who'd already survived one attempt on her life.

He couldn't believe that Robbie hadn't told him about the murder attempt, or that he hadn't heard gossip through some mutual old friend or classmate. But Robbie was nothing if not honorable; if he gave his word that he wouldn't tell anyone, he wouldn't. As for old friends and classmates, Russ hadn't stayed in regular touch with anyone outside of family. He hadn't done much of anything in the past three years besides work and resent the hell out of Jamie and Melinda.

"I don't even know where you live."

He glanced at her, seeing only the back of her head as she stared out the side window. "Not many people do."

"And you like it that way."

"Yeah." Russ liked his privacy, even if it did seem damn lonely at times.

A mile or so passed before he spoke again. "What happened in Macon…" Tommy had used the same phrase. It sounded innocent and harmless. So much better than *getting stabbed four times by a lunatic who wanted you dead.* "Why did you hide it?"

Finally she glanced at him, but her gaze shifted away quickly. "I didn't hide it. I just didn't call attention to it. I didn't want pity. I didn't want people to look at me and see a victim."

I wasn't just "people," he wanted to point

out. They'd been friends. Hell, they'd slept together for all of one semester and half of the next. They'd still been friends when it happened, until she'd come to Copper Lake and agreed to represent Melinda—and *mis*-represent him—in the divorce.

"You don't give people much credit, do you?"

"I didn't leave Macon right away. I went through physical therapy and rehabilitation. I even went back to work in the same firm in the same office. I saw the curiosity and the sympathy and the pity. I answered the endless questions. I gave all the gory details until I just couldn't give them anymore. When I moved here, I wanted to forget. I wanted to be normal again."

Could you forget almost dying in your own office? And if she'd been attacked at night in her office there, why the hell did she work nights in her office here?

To prove to herself that she could. That Shan Davis's father couldn't change the way she lived.

He admired it at the same time he thought it was stupid. No one in Copper Lake gave a damn whether she worked late alone in her office. No one would think less of her, even without knowing her history, for refusing to do so.

Two and a half miles past the turnoff for his mother's house, Russ slowed, then checked the rearview mirror. His was the only vehicle on the road and had been since leaving the city limits. No one had followed them, and no one could possibly know to be waiting along the dirt roads that led to his house. Some of the tension gathered in his neck eased as he turned off the highway.

When he was a kid, the trees had grown in straight lines, evenly spaced, and the under-growth had been kept relatively cleared. But Granddad had quit logging this section twenty years ago, letting it return to its natural state. It was a good place to hike and hunt, and Russ had spent plenty of hours doing just that. He knew every rise, every clearing and thicket, and could follow the banks of Holigan Creek blindfolded. He might get a little lonely, but living out there was worth it. This was where he felt at home.

The logging roads had been laid out in a grid, originally wide enough for two trucks to pass. They were narrower now, the forest encroaching, tree branches forming a canopy overhead in places. The roads they passed were mostly unused, though any number of them would get a person to his house if he knew where it was. It was Russ's goal for them to grow over entirely, disappearing, surrounding him with forest.

For a long time, it had been his goal to disappear himself. To shut out everyone and everything until nothing could touch him again. But his family hadn't let that happen. They were stubborn when they set their minds to something.

"Every intersection looks the same." Across the cab, Jamie gestured as they crossed yet another road. "How does anyone find their way around?"

"They're not the same. You just have to know what to look for."

"It's a little spooky out here. The road getting narrower and overgrown. The trees. No lights. No neighbors."

"That's why people move to the country. To get away from the lights and the people."

She gave a little sniff. "I like neighbors, thank you."

"They weren't of any help to you tonight, were they?"

The dim lights from the dash shadowed her face as her expression darkened. He wished he hadn't said anything. Relieved by the distraction, he made the last turn, negotiated a bumpy hundred yards, then rounded a curve. His house sat in the clearing ahead, illuminated by his headlights and a lone lamp next to the garage.

"Oh, it's pretty."

Her surprise irritated him. "Everything I build looks good. That's part of the job."

She gave him an admonishing look. "I didn't mean that. It just looks like the perfect family home. A yard, flowers, a porch swing."

And he wasn't the family type. Not anymore.

Scowling, he parked in front of the garage, then got out and circled the truck to unload her bags from the back. He normally entered through the garage, but this time he followed the stone path to the porch, fished the house key from the ring and unlocked the front door, then stepped back so she could enter first.

The only light burning was a lamp in the family room, straight ahead at the back of the house. It was enough to see that the place was neat and clean, that he hadn't left castoff clothes or dishes lying around as he often did. Not that it mattered. Jamie wasn't a guest. He wasn't looking to impress her.

He was just trying to keep her safe.

Chapter 4

The house wasn't overly large or ostentatious, though Russ could easily afford both, but it was lovely. Jamie set her bags on the stone floor of the entry, then moved farther into the family room. Rough-hewn beams arched overhead, the shape echoed in the stone fireplace that dominated one wall. The floors past the foyer were wood, broad planks that looked a hundred years old, and the walls were painted a bold hunter-green. Tall windows flanked the fireplace, looking out into the dark night, and soapstone lined the counters and the island that marked the kitchen to the right.

The chairs and sofa were distressed leather, the tables solid oak, the rugs homey and showing the signs of heavy wear. Family heirlooms, she'd bet, passed down through generations of Calloways.

It was a good thing he'd waited until Melinda was gone to build the house, or she would have done her best to get it, too. Not that the house she'd been given in the divorce and immediately sold had been any too shabby. She had just been greedy. She'd wanted it all.

Jamie had wanted it all, too, though her definition had varied tremendously. A husband, kids, a home. Melinda's husband, to be exact. And now here she was, a guest in his home.

She might have been safer at a motel.

He set her bigger bags next to the small ones, then went past her and into the kitchen, switching on lights as he went. "Have you eaten?"

"Yes." Another frozen dinner that had made

Mischa turn up her nose. Thought of the dog made her stomach clench. She pulled her cell phone from her purse and was scrolling through the directory for the vet's number when Russ spoke again.

"Cell service out here is hit-or-miss. There's a phone on the desk."

The cell's power signal was at its lowest. With a nod, she crossed to the desk at the far end of the room from the kitchen. It was massive, oak with brass pulls, and bore the signs of a long life of hard work. She remembered it well—one of only a few pieces of furniture in his house in Athens that had made the trip from home with him. It had belonged to Cyrus Calloway, his ancestor who'd founded Copper Lake two hundred years ago. She sat in the wooden chair with its leather cushion and dialed the vet's number while the mouthwatering aromas of sweet onions sizzling and ground beef grilling filled the air.

Dr. Yates couldn't tell her anything new—

just that Mischa was okay and still sleeping. She thanked him, hung up, then swiveled the chair so she could stand. Instead, she sat a moment, watching Russ. He moved around the kitchen with the familiarity of someone who spent a good deal of time there. Back when they were together, he'd been even less adept at cooking than she was. He'd stored beer in his refrigerator, cookies and chips in the cabinets and had the take-out menus for every restaurant in town. Later, Melinda hadn't liked eating at home. She'd married one of the town's favored sons, and she reminded people of it every chance she got. They'd been regulars at the country club and every other decent restaurant in town.

Jamie hadn't cared about prestige or flaunting her catch. She'd just wanted Russ, while Melinda had wanted what he could give her. And he'd wanted Melinda. It wasn't fair.

If she hadn't learned that life wasn't fair a hundred times over growing up, she would have figured it out when Russ dumped her for Melinda, or when Harlan Davis attacked her.

Because watching him wasn't the best thing for her mental health, she rose from the chair and shifted her attention to the fireplace. A rugged beam served as mantel, and above it hung a family portrait, taken sometime after Gerald Calloway's death. Sara sat in the middle, surrounded by her sons and Mitch, wearing a smile of utter contentment. It was the same smile Mitch's wife, Jessica, wore, the same as Rick's wife, Amanda's, but for very different reasons.

"She never looked that happy when the old man was alive." Russ stopped a few yards away, munching on a napkin-wrapped burger. He liked them rare, Jamie recalled. With sauteed onions, mustard, pickles and ketchup, while she preferred hers well-done. Like shoe leather, he'd teased.

"An awful lot of people are happier without their spouse than with," she said carefully, watching peripherally for his reaction.

Any change in his expression was too guarded to catch. It wasn't necessary anyway. She knew he wasn't one of those. He'd loved his wife. In some ways, he probably still did.

"The guest rooms are this way." He led the way past the desk and into a hallway that ran front to back, opening into the foyer at the opposite end. There was a bedroom in front and another in back with a bathroom in between. The rooms were similar, one painted taupe, one pale green, each filled with mismatched antiques and large windows that let in the night.

Ordinarily she didn't mind such openness. The three sets of French doors that led to her patio were covered with only the filmiest of curtains, offering no privacy at all when the lights were on inside. But this was as far from an ordinary night as she'd seen in three and a half years. At least these windows, unlike the family room, had blinds she could lower and close so she could cower without any chance of curious eyes seeing.

The thought of someone out there in the darkness made her shiver, but she masked it with a shrug as she chose the rear room. The green on the walls was soothing, and the old-fashioned bed, high off the floor and piled with pillows, reminded her of her grand-mother's guest room where she'd spent many a night as a kid. Everything had always been perfect at Gran's, and she could use a little of that illusion tonight.

"Where is your room?" she asked as she headed for the foyer to get her bags. It was going to feel weird enough staying the night in a strange house, even weirder knowing it was Russ's house. It would help to know where he would be if she got up in the night.

If she needed his protection.

He looked as if the thought had occurred to him, as well. "On the other side of the kitchen."

"You can go ahead and finish your dinner. I'll get my bags and, uh, get ready for bed."

Easing past him, she took the hall in long strides. She was pretty sure he stood there near the door and watched until she was out of sight, but when she returned a moment later, laden with her bags, he was gone.

She hung the garment bag in the closet and set out the few toiletries she would need tonight in the bathroom, but left everything else in the bags. It wasn't as if she was staying more than a day or two. She couldn't imagine Russ's generosity or her own nerves lasting any longer than that. After washing the makeup from her face, she changed into her pajamas—cotton shorts and a tank top—then returned to the bedroom.

With the blinds lowered and twisted tightly shut, the room seemed cozier. It smelled faintly of hazelnut, though not from any source within the room. It was coffee brewing in the kitchen, perfuming the air. She didn't drink coffee herself, though she'd developed a taste for Russ's postcoffee kisses. Back when she'd been young and hopeful and he hadn't broken her heart and no one had tried to kill her.

Pretending it was any normal night, she snuggled into bed, fat pillows behind her and a puffy comforter pulled to her waist, and opened the magazine she'd grabbed from her night table. Usually, she'd had such a day that a few articles were enough to put her to sleep. Not tonight. Oh, she read the articles. She just couldn't focus. Couldn't make sense of the words. She wasn't even sure she was seeing the right words, partly because her eyes were watering, partly because her hands were trembling. Hell, her whole body was trembling.

Shoving back the covers, she slid from the bed. She knew this antsy feeling. Sometimes it grabbed hold of her just before the verdict was announced in a particularly important case. The first time she'd walked back into her Macon office after the attack, she'd been so anxious that she'd forgotten to breathe. The first time she'd faced Russ as Melinda's lawyer, she'd been sick from the inside out. There was nothing to do but wait it out, though activity did usually help. If she were home, she'd hit the treadmill in the guest room. If Robbie were home, she'd call him to go for a walk along the river with her. He would complain, but he would do it. If things were different with Russ, she'd jump his bones. That would make her forget.

Stifling a bitter laugh, she opened the door and listened. The living room was dimly lit. There were no sounds, no television, no utensils against dishes, and the fragrance of the hazelnut was fading. Russ had probably gone to his room, maybe to bed. He'd always been an early riser.

Arms hugging her middle, she eased around the corner, saw that the room was empty, with only one lamp burning, and walked farther in. The wood floor was cool beneath her feet as she moved along the perimeter of the room.

Paintings of serious value—more family heirlooms—hung on two walls, while photographs of his family and friends filled in the spaces between. A set of six-foot-tall glass-fronted barrister bookcases, the shelves packed with books, marked the end of the display area, then the kitchen proper began. The cabinets were oak, the pulls antiqued brass. With the soapstone counters and...

The sound of running water stopped her mid-ramble. Russ was in the shower. There was an image she didn't need, one she'd seen often enough before he'd met Melinda. Water hot enough to steam, smooth tanned flesh, hair sleek against his head, muscles flexing, skin glistening... Just the memory had the power to make her hot, to dry her mouth and make her hungry.

Abruptly the water shut off. She imagined him stepping out, reaching for a towel, dripping on the rug beneath his feet. Swallowing hard, she forced herself to move. But instead of rushing back to her room, she went to the cabinets, searching for a glass. She needed cold water before she ignited inside.

"What are you looking for?"

Her hand stilled, her fingers closing around the pull on the third cabinet door. There was no way he'd dried off and dressed that fast. Granted, his hair was so short that it needed just a swipe or two with a towel to soak up the excess water, but still… "Glasses," she managed to answer without sounding strangled.

"Next door over. There's pop, beer and bottled water in the refrigerator."

She shook her head. "I just need a drink." After taking a glass from the bottom shelf, she closed the door, then steeled herself to turn.

She'd been right. He hadn't had time to dry off and get dressed. He wore a thick towel knotted around his waist, and drops of water dampened his shoulders, arms and chest. She dropped her gaze to the floor—safer territory—and saw that his feet were still damp, too.

She had to pass him to get to the refrigerator. There was plenty of room, but it felt much too confined. She hadn't been with a man in a long time, hadn't been with this man in a very long time, and this wasn't a normal night. She needed activity. Distraction.

He rinsed his coffee cup, then set it in the dishwasher while she filled the glass with ice, then water. For her own protection—or was it his?—she went to stand on the opposite side of the island, sipping the water before commenting. "You're the only person I know who can drink a cup of coffee and be asleep in five minutes."

He shrugged, skin rippling. "Caffeine never has kept me awake."

"You still sleep like a rock?"

"Yeah."

Her smile was unsteady. "I'll remember that. If I have to scream, I'll scream loudly."

He didn't return the smile. "No one followed us here."

She nodded. She'd seen him watching the rearview mirrors all the way from her house.

"This is the last place anyone would expect you to go. They'd check the motels first, then maybe Lys's."

"Should I warn her?" All this time she'd been worried about Mischa, about herself, and hadn't given any thought to Lys's safety. Everyone in town knew they were best friends, and a stranger could find out easily enough. Lys lived alone in her half of a duplex, though the other half was shared by two of Copper Lake's hunkiest firemen. If they were off duty, they would come running at the first hint of trouble. *If* they were off duty.

Russ shrugged. "Call her if you want. But block the number, and don't tell her where you are."

"Why not?"

"Because Tommy said not to. Hiding isn't hiding once you start telling people where you are."

"But Lys—"

He shrugged again, clearly not caring.

Jamie took another drink of water, shivering as the icy liquid hit the back of her throat, then went to the desk. She had to look in the phone book for instructions on how to block the number. She was a regular person. She didn't try to hide from people.

She was halfway through a message when Lys picked up. Jamie kept the conversation intentionally vague, though it was hard, especially when Lys asked the inevitable question. "Where are you?"

Especially with Russ watching. "I—I can't say."

There was stunned silence on the line before Lys found her voice. "You can't—Jamie, this is *me*. Associate, employee, *friend?* What do you mean, you can't say?"

"Tommy Maricci told me not to."

Lys snorted scornfully. "Tommy Maricci never would have *made* detective if it wasn't for his friendship with the Calloways. Hell, if it wasn't for them, he would be *in* jail instead of trying to put other people there."

That wasn't true—Tommy was a good cop—but Jamie didn't argue with her. Keeping her voice steady, she said, "I'll be in the office in the morning, as usual. Just…be careful. If anything weird happens tonight, call the police." Before Lys could protest, she hung up.

"There's a bottle of aspirin in the top left drawer," Russ said.

"I don't have a headache."

"Lys always gives people a pain somewhere."

Pushing to her feet, Jamie returned to the island. "You don't like her much, do you?"

"I don't like her at all."

"Did you used to date her?" Jamie had always assumed a good deal of Lys's antagonism toward Russ was based on her own rocky relationship with him, but that was arrogant.

He and Lys had grown up in the same town, though he was six or eight years older than her. She could have had plenty of contact with him before Jamie came to town, could have come by that antagonism completely on her own.

"Yeah, right, me and freaky Lys." He moved to lean against the counter, ankles crossed. "I never dated anyone seriously until Melinda."

Jamie's breath caught in her chest, and the floor seemed to sink out from under her. Feeling sore inside, she took one last drink of water, grateful she didn't choke on it, then eased the glass onto the counter. "I think I'll go to bed now."

Moving carefully and quietly, she returned to the guest room, closed the door and sat down on the edge of the bed. It was so high that only her toes touched the floor, pressing against the braided rug there.

She'd been in love with Russ six years ago, and she'd thought that he might have loved her, too. At the least, she'd believed he cared about her. Oh, she knew he'd gotten over her. He'd married Melinda, after all, and had been obscenely happy with her in the beginning. But he'd cared about Jamie first. He'd maybe-loved Jamie first. She'd found some comfort in that.

But she'd been wrong. He'd never even been serious about her. She'd just been a way to pass the time while he waited for the real love of his life to come along. He'd used her, fooled her, never cared about her at all.

She sat there a long time, not moving, not seeing, not thinking, until finally exhaustion claimed her. Sliding under the covers, warmed with her own body heat, she wondered if it was possible to not feel.

She damn sure intended to try.

Russ woke before six to the aroma of dark Colombian coffee brewing in the next room. He pulled on a T-shirt over his boxers, then headed for the kitchen for a jolt of caffeine and a toaster pastry.

The first thing he saw when he rounded the corner by the refrigerator was a pair of long bare legs. He damn near skidded to a stop, abruptly remembering. The dog, the stalker, Jamie. She was standing at the near end of the island, a book open in front of her—an old yearbook—and a bottle of water beside her. She still wore her pajamas, shorts and a top that were damn near indecent, and her hair fell in a tangle past her shoulders. No makeup, hardly any clothes and not even a finger-comb through her hair, and she still looked... How had Robbie described her the other day? As a living, breathing goddess?

No, those were *his* words, before he'd known who they were talking about. But pretty damn accurate all the same. Her legs were long, lean, and her ass, jutted out as she bent over the island, was damn fine. Nice waist, better-than-nice breasts, a few freckles dotting her cheeks and nose...

Aw, jeez, this was *Jamie.* Satan. Queen of the

damned. The last thing in the world he wanted was to feel anything even remotely positive toward her.

No, the *last* thing he wanted was for anything to happen to her. Especially if he could prevent it.

She was reaching for a section of peeled orange from the napkin next to her water when he finally forced one foot forward, then the other. She glanced at him, her expression utterly blank, said a polite good morning, then turned her attention back to the yearbook.

He got his coffee, added milk and sugar and put two sugar-frosted Danish in the toaster before finally gesturing to the book with his mug. "You like looking at old pictures?"

She straightened. Too bad. "I like seeing how people have changed."

He didn't want to think about how he'd changed since high school. He'd been naive back then. With the exception of his loser father, life had been pretty good, and he'd stupidly thought it would always be that way.

"Robbie still looks the same."

He moved close enough to see the picture she was pointing at. Robbie, sophomore class president, wearing the grin that got him both into and out of more trouble than any three kids combined.

"So do you." She flipped back through the pages, past the junior class, to the beginning of the senior class pictures, tapping his photo. Her fingers were long and slim, the nails rounded and polished.

He hardly glanced at the photograph. "It's been a lot of years."

"Only fourteen."

"In calendar time. Not in real time." He'd aged a lot more than fourteen years since that picture had been taken, most of it in the past three years. Disillusionment had a way of doing that to people.

Using the toaster as an excuse to back off, he

retreated to the other end of the kitchen, fishing out the hot pastries, dropping each piece on a saucer. Had *she* been disillusioned when her client's father tried to kill her? A thing like that could make a person go into seclusion, could make it damn near impossible to trust anyone again.

But she hadn't. She'd moved to a whole new place, where she knew only him and Robbie. She'd started over. She'd made friends. She hadn't turned her house into a fortified camp. Hadn't started carrying a gun or been afraid to move about.

Four stab wounds, Jamie had said. Picturing her clearly even though his back was to her, he wondered where. He hadn't seen any scars, not that he'd gotten to look as closely as he'd have liked. Given her history, it was a wonder she hadn't turned tail and run the other night when…

His face went scarlet, and he choked down the food in his mouth before turning. "When

I pulled out that knife Wednesday night…I didn't know…I didn't mean… Jeez."

She shrugged as if the incident hadn't bothered her at all. "I knew you would never use it on me."

Knew how? His behavior since the divorce had been crappy. On the few occasions in the beginning, when she'd tried to be friendly, he hadn't even managed civil. He'd been so damn angry. How could she *know* anything about what he would or wouldn't have done?

Still, the conviction in her voice made him feel less of a bastard.

A little less.

"What time do you usually go to work?" he asked, pulling out a barstool at the end of the island and sitting down with his coffee and breakfast.

"The office opens at nine, but any time's okay. What time do you usually go?"

"I'm already on my way most days." But most days he didn't have an overnight guest.

In fact, she was the first person to stay over in this house.

She polished off the last of the orange and wiped her hands on the napkin. "I can be ready in fifteen minutes."

"You don't have to—"

"The earlier you drop me off, the less likely anyone will see us." She returned the yearbook to the bottom shelf of the bookcase and lowered the glass door. He got one look of snug-fitting cotton stretched across her butt as she bent, and dropped his gaze to his breakfast. Suddenly it seemed too hot for steaming coffee and pastry, though in reality both had cooled to little more than warm.

Hell.

He finished the first pastry, then returned to the bedroom to pull on jeans and boots. After brushing his teeth, he tucked his shirt in, then zipped up. He was back at the island, finishing the second pastry, when she returned.

She wore snug-fitting gray pants and darker

gray heels that made her legs look a mile long, with a light-purple top and a matching sweater. Her hair was pulled back in a ponytail, then clipped up on her head, leaving the ends to fall back down, and she'd put on makeup. She didn't need it. She was pretty enough without it.

Grinding his teeth at the thought, he poured his coffee into a travel mug, grabbed his cell phone from the charger and clipped it to his belt. He was halfway to the door when he reversed, returning to his bedroom. When he came back with a zippered padded case in hand, Jamie's gaze fixed on it for a moment. The attack on her might not have made her hypercautious, but she recognized the gun rug for what it was. She didn't comment on it, though, and neither did he.

The morning was cool, the humidity high. It promised to be another muggy, hot day, not ideal for outdoor work, but better than an office anytime.

As Russ stopped to lock the double-keyed dead bolt, Jamie walked to the edge of the porch. "Do you ever sit outside and just enjoy the day?"

He glanced at the swing on one side of the door, the oak rockers on the other side, and shook his head. "I don't have time." His house was his refuge…but he suspected it wouldn't feel quite so good if he spent too much time there. It would give him too many chances to think about how different life was supposed to have been. So he worked instead. A lot.

The drive into town was silent. He drank his coffee and watched the traffic, and she sat motionless in the passenger seat, staring off into the distance. There were few cars on the highway, and not many more once they reached town. Morning rush hour in Copper Lake lasted all of five minutes, so there were no early commuters.

"Do you have a key to the back door of your building?" Russ asked as he turned at the square.

Jamie glanced at him blankly, then dug her keys from her purse. "Yes."

He drove to the end of the block, turned right toward the tiny parking lot carved out behind her building. He parked in the space nearest her door and climbed out. She didn't protest as she got out.

"I never park back here," she commented. "The only time the sun hits it is high noon, and at night it's downright creepy."

"Good place for a stalker to hide."

She cut him a look, then wiggled the key into the lock and twisted it. The door opened with a spook-house creak into a narrow space, where another door opened into the foyer. He followed her to her office, into reception, then into her private office. Everything was quiet. Normal, judging by her actions.

Russ pulled a business card from his hip pocket and offered it to her. His phone numbers—cell, office and home—were on it. "Call me when freaky Lys leaves this evening."

Again, she didn't protest, though she looked

like she wanted to this time. Instead, she tucked the business card under the edge of the desk pad and absently said, "Don't call her that."

He stood near the door, ready to leave but feeling as if he should say something. But what? *Be careful?* She knew that. *Watch your back?* She knew that now, too. Instead, he shrugged and left, locking the doors behind him as he went.

At eight-thirty, fifteen minutes before her usual time, Lys blew into the office like a hurricane. She was clearly upset, but not too upset to make her usual stop for doughnuts and diet pop. Before she set the box and the cans on the desk, she demanded, "Are you all right?"

"I'm fine."

"And Mischa?"

"She's fine, too." Jamie had called Dr. Yates as soon as Russ left and gotten a good report. He was waiting on the tox screen, but Mischa had slept comfortably all night, had already made a trip outside and had been settling down to breakfast as they spoke. Whatever drug she'd been given, she seemed to be suffering no ill effects.

Ignoring the doughnuts once she'd opened the box, Lys sat back and crossed her legs, then her arms. Today she was dressed all in white—a slim-fitting sheath that stopped midthigh with four-inch strappy heels. White wasn't an obvious choice for her coloring, but somehow, like the solid black from the day before, she made it look good, even with the deep-red-with-purple-undertones lipstick that matched her nails.

"I didn't see the rental outside. How did you get to work this morning?"

Jamie stuffed half a glazed doughnut in her mouth, then lifted her shoulders in a shrug.

"I bet Maricci brought you. Where did you stay last night?"

Still using the food as an excuse, Jamie shrugged again.

"Come and stay with me. I know, you don't want to put me in any danger, but that's not a problem. I'm not afraid of this guy, whoever he is. You and I together will kick his ass."

Finally Jamie had no choice but to swallow. "I can't, Lys. It's too risky. And you *should* be afraid. You know Mischa. What kind of scum would hurt her?" Before Lys could say anything, she rushed on. "I appreciate the offer, really, I do. But we're both safer if no one knows where I am. You can always reach me on my cell phone." Service might not be reliable out in the woods, but she could use Russ's phone to check for voice mails.

"But, Jamie—"

Hating her tone, part pout, part plea, Jamie interrupted. "The garage in Augusta called after we left last night. My car's ready. Would it be possible for you to return the rental and pick it up today? I'd go, but I don't think Tommy would approve."

Lys sat in silence for a moment, then grudgingly nodded. "For once, I'd agree with him. Too many places between here and Augusta for something to go wrong."

"You're right. Forget I asked you. I'll find someone else—"

"No one's going to mistake me for you. Beyond the fact that we're both female, we have nothing else in common. I'll go this morning. Where is the rental?" There was a bit of curiosity in her eyes, as if she hoped Jamie had driven to wherever she'd spent the night.

"It's in my driveway. Probably smells of Mischa."

"How the hell did you get her into the car by yourself?"

"I didn't." Though one doughnut contained more than enough calories for one day's breakfast, Jamie fished out another and took a bite, mumbling through it. "Actually, Russ Calloway was working at the Petrovskis'. He helped."

Eyes wide-open, Lys stared at her. "He just happens to 'find' the nail strip behind your tire, and then he's 'working' in your neighborhood at the same time Mischa gets poisoned? You don't think that's a little too coincidental?"

"No. I don't."

"Jamie, he hates you. He's avoided you for three years, but now, when things start going wrong, suddenly he's there every time you turn around? Come on. So you used to be in love with him. That was years ago. He's not the same guy anymore."

She'd been in love with a man whom she'd thought loved her back. He'd *never* been that guy, Jamie thought morosely. She'd been wrong about him then. Could she be wrong now?

No. Certain things were just inarguable facts. Grass was green, water was wet and Russ was *not* the kind of guy who'd stalk a woman. Even if he did hate her.

Rather than argue with Lys, she simply said nothing.

Rolling her eyes, Lys got to her feet, chose

a doughnut from the box and headed for the door. "I'll go through the messages and the e-mail, then pick up the rental and head for Augusta. The county bar's monthly dinner is tonight at the country club. I assume you'll want to skip that." She glanced over her shoulder into the outer office, then said, voice dripping sarcasm, "Maricci's here."

"That's Detective Maricci to you, Paxton."

With another roll of her eyes, Lys went to her desk. Tommy came inside and closed the door. He wore snug-fitting jeans and a blue polo shirt embroidered with the Copper Lake Police Department seal. "So you survived the night."

"Did you think I wouldn't?" Jamie asked dryly.

"It occurred to me that one of you might kill the other. I'd've put my money on you strangling him, though. Anything new I should know about?"

"We had a quiet uneventful night."

"Yeah, so did I. I usually do when I get called out in the middle of a date."

"Sorry my stalker interfered with your social life."

He shrugged magnanimously. "Who needs a social life? I know a number of people who get by just fine without one. You, Russ…"

Jamie gave him a surprised look as she rose from her desk. "I have a social life."

He snorted. "When's the last time you went out? And Robbie and Lys don't count. Robbie's like your best girlfriend, and Lys is freaky."

"Don't call her that." She swung open the heavy vault door and gestured to the strip of wood on top of a file cabinet.

Tommy made notes on an adhesive evidence seal, scooped the strip into a paper bag using a napkin from the desk, then sealed the fold with the label. "We'll need to get fingerprints from you and Lys to rule you out. I got Russ's this morning." He looked back at her. "So? Last date?"

"I don't remember."

"Since me?"

"Maybe not." She and Tommy had gone out to dinner once. They'd had a nice time, he'd kissed her good night, and they'd decided to be friends.

"I know I broke your heart, but you're too young and pretty to live life alone."

She imitated his snort. "Sorry to disappoint you, but my heart is intact." More or less. More than six years ago, maybe a little less than twenty-four hours ago.

"Listen." That quickly Tommy turned serious. "The only prints on the note from last night were Russ's. We haven't gotten anything on the flowers or the candy, but we're looking. I checked on the Davises. They're both still in prison. Between them, they've had maybe three visitors since they went in. My gut says this doesn't involve them."

"So that leaves someone local."

"Anyone ask you out that you turned down?"

Because she liked the closeness and security of the vault too much for her own comfort, Jamie returned to her desk. "A number of guys, but no one who cared enough to try to change my mind."

"Make a list for me, will you?"

She pulled a notepad and pen from her desk drawer and began writing. She hated pointing a finger at men who were very likely innocent, hated the doubts and the wariness and the suspicion. But not as much as she hated the fear.

It was a short list—six names. Tommy scanned it, then folded it and stuck it in his hip pocket. "Okay, so we know who likes you. Who doesn't like you?"

Russ. But she wouldn't say it out loud. *Wouldn't.*

"Besides the obvious," Tommy added grimly. "Have you defended anybody here in town who's gone to jail?"

She shook her head. "I don't take major criminal cases. Just misdemeanors."

"Anyone get a raw deal in a civil case?" Again, he added, "Besides the obvious."

"I'm not comfortable discussing my clients," she said stiffly.

"You weren't comfortable taking your dog to the vet last night, either."

"I don't have any ideas. Honestly. I've hardly gotten used to the idea that I've got a stalker. I can't begin to think who it could be."

Tommy studied her a moment, then nodded. "Okay. Someone will come over to take your prints. Other than that, stay alert. Let me know if anything comes up. Here's my cell phone number." He flipped a card onto her desk. It spun three hundred and sixty degrees in midair and landed, right side up, in the middle of the desk pad. With a grin and a wink, he left.

"Hey, Paxton," she heard from the outer office. "We need your prints. Don't leave town till we get them."

Friends fingerprinted, potential dates investigated…how had her life come to this?

Chapter 5

It was 5:55 p.m. when Russ's cell phone rang. He slid it from his waistband and flipped it open. "Calloway."

"It's Jamie. Lys is gone, so whenever you're ready…" She sounded tired. It had been a longer day than usual, and probably a tougher one. Having the cops come by, asking a lot of questions and taking your fingerprints wasn't anyone's idea of fun, not even when it was Tommy.

"I'll meet you at the back door in ten

minutes." He hung up before she could say anything else and walked through the building until he located his foreman. "I'm heading out. If you need anything, you can reach me on the cell or at home."

Ken Martin's eyes widened. "You're going home? It's not even six o'clock. I can't remember the last time you quit work before six o'clock."

"That's because you're a slacker who thinks ten-hour days are long enough. I'll see you Monday."

The condos were going up on the west side of the river, each with a view of the water, downtown and River's Edge. They snaked along the riverbank, backing up to tennis courts and a golf course, and would be modern and high-tech inside while looking on the outside as if they'd been there a hundred years.

Sometimes he felt as if he'd been working on them a hundred years. He was glad to be leaving, glad to be going home.

And it didn't have a damn thing to do with his houseguest. He hadn't given her a thought all day. Well, except when Tommy had caught up with him this morning. And when he'd seen Lys driving the convertible. And when he'd taken a break for lunch at the deli. And when he'd stopped by River's Edge... Hell and damnation.

He drove into downtown and turned into the alley behind Jamie's office. Before he had a chance to get out, the rear door to the building opened and she came out, locked up, then headed his way.

There wasn't anything deliberate about the way she moved—it was just her usual walk— but there *was* something about it, something feminine, something... He didn't want to say the word, didn't want to even think it in connection with Jamie, but the sway of her hips, the flex of muscle, the faint movement of her breasts...

Sexy.

She climbed into the truck, settled her purse

on the seat and the briefcase on the floor, then
fastened her seat belt. Her only greeting was
a hesitant smile. His was a curt nod.

He turned around and pulled back onto the
street, but instead of heading toward home, he
went east. When she glanced his way, he said,
"We're going by Yancy's. He said Mischa
could go home."

Surprise crossed her face. "You don't
mind?"

Could having a ninety-pound dog in his
house be any more distracting than having
Jamie there? He couldn't imagine it.

Mischa was ecstatic about seeing Jamie,
dragging Yancy along by the leash, lunging at
her owner, who'd had the sense to brace herself
against the counter. The dog wiggled and
shivered all over while Jamie cooed to her, then,
greeting finished, Mischa headed for the door.

"Here, Russ, make yourself useful," Yancy
said, handing the looped end of the leash to
him. "Walk her around the grass a bit."

Scowling, Russ took the leash, then opened the door. Mischa didn't seem to know any commands. She jerked him here and there as she sniffed along the grass before finding a good spot under a tree to relieve herself. That done, she turned abruptly to look at him, as if she'd just realized she was in the company of a stranger. Her dark eyes narrowed and the patch of hair between her shoulders bristled. A low growl rumbled up from inside her, ending quickly when Jamie and Yancy came out of the clinic. Mischa ran to Jamie, and Russ gladly surrendered the leash to her, then took the twenty-pound bag of dog food Yancy offered and tossed it into the truck bed.

The dog made the cab seem a lot more crowded. She sat on the seat between him and Jamie, panting excitedly, breaking off on occasion to look at Russ and display her teeth. She didn't growl again, though, until Russ reached out to adjust the air conditioner.

"Mischa! Bad girl." Jamie gave her collar a

tug. "She never gets aggressive with anyone. She's just a big baby."

As if to prove it, Mischa dropped to her side, laid her head in Jamie's lap and stretched, her huge feet pushing hard against his leg. Wearing a wolfish grin as Jamie scratched her, she looked at him and curled her lip back from her teeth.

Great. He was spending the weekend with Satan and the hound of Satan. This ought to be fun.

They were halfway home when the dog went to sleep, her snores sounding remarkably like Robbie's, just louder. Russ glanced across her to Jamie. "What did Yancy say about the drug?"

"It was a sedative, commonly used, the dosage calculated for her size."

"So the intent was to scare you, not to harm her."

She nodded grimly.

"The guy wrote her name on the note. Who knows her?"

"My friends, my neighbors. I take her for

walks through the neighborhood and down by the river pretty regularly, and we see the same people. Everyone at Dr. Yates's office knows her." She shrugged. "A lot of people."

"And anyone who's been watching you at home." The houses on her street sat two hundred feet back from the curb, and there were plenty of trees and bushes where someone could take cover. What kind of sick bastard hid in the dark and watched a woman alone?

The same kind who drugged a dog just to scare its owner.

He slowed to make a turn from one logging road to another. "I saw Lys driving your car today. Where has it been?"

"In a garage in Augusta. Something with the transmission."

Not something a stalker could have done. Just bad luck and coincidence.

Still scratching the dog's neck, Jamie asked, "Could we not talk about this right now? It gets a little overwhelming."

"Yeah, sure."

They were silent the rest of the way home.

After the dog ran around the yard, doing a frenzied sniff-and-piss job, they went inside. Mischa trotted ahead, checking out everything along the way. She sniffed along the sofa, one of the chairs, then paid meticulous attention to the chair where Russ usually sat. Tongue out, she climbed into it, turned a couple of times, then dropped down.

"Mischa," Jamie started to scold, but the dog closed her eyes and breathed loudly, mimicking her own snores. "I'm sorry. I made a mistake in letting her on the furniture in the beginning. She likes to be comfortable, and I'm a bad disciplinarian."

Russ stifled a snort. Choosing that chair had nothing to do with comfort. The dog had claimed it because it was his, and as long as she was sitting in it, he couldn't.

Could have been worse. She could have peed on it.

"It's okay," he said, laying his cell phone and the gun rug on the island. "I'm going to take a shower, then I'll fix dinner."

He went to his room and into the bathroom, closing the door behind him. The privacy didn't make him forget that there was someone else in his house. That she was probably headed for the guest room, where she would probably take off those clothes, maybe let down her hair and put on something more casual. He'd vote for the skimpy pajamas, even if bedtime was three or four hours away.

Not that he cared as he turned on the shower to hot. No matter what she wore, she was still Jamie. Ex-friend and scum-sucking lawyer. She was still Melinda's partner in crime.

And none of that changed the fact that she was still pretty. Still sexy. That he still remembered the good times they'd had back in school.

The sex between them had been the best of those good times.

Until Melinda. Meeting her had knocked him on his ass. Six years later he still regretted it.

He kept the water hot enough to steam and scrubbed off the day's work and sweat. He didn't want to think about Melinda, or all the sex he hadn't had since the divorce, or how good all the sex he *had* had with Jamie had been. He didn't want to think about Jamie, either, but since she was in his house, that seemed unavoidable.

He'd dried off and pulled on boxers when the phone beside the bed rang. Caller ID showed Robbie's cell, so he picked up, bracing the phone between his ear and shoulder while stepping into a clean pair of jeans. "Hey, bubba, how's the fishing?"

"Worth coming down here for. How're things there?"

"Okay."

Robbie waited a moment, then said, "Aw, come on. Mischa got drugged, you saved the day and took Satan home with you, and all you have to say is 'okay?'"

The back of Russ's neck prickled with the nickname. Yeah, he'd resented Jamie like hell, but maybe he should have kept it to himself. Right, and then one day he would have exploded. "How do you know I brought her here?"

"Tommy told me."

"Huh. He told us not to tell anyone."

"I'm not just 'anyone.' I'm the most important guy in Jamie's life."

That made Russ's neck prickle, too. Most people in town assumed Robbie and Jamie were secretly sleeping together, the kind of no-strings-attached affair that would end when someone better came along for one of them. Russ had never thought that, though. Robbie being friends with his enemy was one thing. Sleeping with her, especially when Russ had slept with her first, was something way different.

But Robbie had never actually said they were platonic. All his flaws aside, he rarely discussed the women in his life. The last time he'd been indiscreet, it had been a combination of way too much booze and the rowdy atmosphere of a strip club, and he'd learned from the experience.

"So how's it going?"

Russ stubbornly repeated the same answer. "Okay."

Robbie muttered a profanity. "Has Tommy found out anything?"

"Sounds like you know as much as we do. He interviewed me. He called it talking, but it was an interview." How often had he been in contact with Jamie, had he known that apricot roses were her favorite, had he remembered that she had a fondness for liqueur-filled chocolates—that sort of stuff. No, Russ hadn't known about the roses or the chocolates. Truth was, he didn't remember much about her likes and dislikes, other than the fact that she would never go to his favorite restaurant with him. He could have eaten Mexican five nights a week, but she'd refused to touch it.

He'd slept with her for more than six months. He should remember more than the facts that she didn't like Mexican food, that she smelled good and that the sex was great.

He would bet she remembered more.

He would bet that she'd cared more.

"So how are you two getting along?"

There was a sly quality to Robbie's voice, but Russ knew how to deal with that. "Okay."

"Damn, bubba... Don't you be mean to her."

Russ's first instinct was to deny that he was ever *mean* to anyone. But when he was angry, he talked to his brother. Robbie had heard every ugly name, every insult and curse a dozen times over. He *had* been mean. Justifiably, but still... "If you're so worried about her, cut your trip short, come home and babysit her yourself."

"I can do that."

Cut a fishing trip short for a platonic friend? Not Robbie. Not any Calloway worthy of the name.

His neck twitchy again, Russ rubbed his hand over it. "Yeah, sure. I'll believe that when I see it. Listen, I've got to get dinner started. If anything comes up, I'll call you."

"Yeah. Tell Jamie I called."

If they *were* more than just friends, wouldn't he want to talk to her, to see for himself that she was all right? Maybe. Maybe not. Russ didn't offer to call her to the phone. He just muttered that he would pass on the message and hung up.

When he went into the kitchen, Jamie was sitting at the island, a bottle of water in front of her. She'd changed clothes, though he'd have to find an excuse to walk around the island to see her outfit. She hadn't let her hair down, though. He'd always liked it down. She'd liked it out of the way.

One more thing he'd remembered. He hadn't been totally self-centered in their months together.

"Can I help with dinner?" she asked as he

opened both refrigerator and freezer to see what was available.

"I don't know. You like spaghetti?"

"Sure."

He pulled a container of sauce from the freezer, then a hunk of mozzarella from the refrigerator. "You can grate that. Grater's in the middle drawer there." Sure, he could have handed it to her, but then she'd have no reason to move away from the counter.

She slid to her feet and walked into the kitchen. Her orange top ended about the same place where khaki shorts started. They were cuffed, pressed and creased, and about five inches too long for his tastes. Her feet were bare, and her toe nails were painted scarlet. Jamie washed her hands, located the grater, a knife and a bowl to grate into, then returned to the barstool. Finally he peeled the lid off the freezer dish, stuck the sauce in the microwave to thaw and placed a pot of water on the stove to heat.

"Robbie called," he said after salting the water and adding a blob of olive oil.

"How's the fishing?"

"Worth going down there for."

She snorted. "Robbie thinks a bad day fishing is better than a good day doing anything else."

"Except having sex."

Jamie's grating paused before starting again. "I wouldn't know about that part."

"You've never slept with him?" The words came out before he realized it and brought a flush of heat to his neck.

The hunk of cheese stilled over the grater again. He stared: the cheese creamy-white, her pale slender fingers holding it delicately, the pinkish-tan nails the only spot of color. Her fingers tensed, then eased, and slowly began moving the cheese back and forth again.

"No, I never have," she said, sounding almost normal. Then her voice darkened. "One Calloway was enough for me."

He raised his gaze to her face then. Her forehead was lined, her mouth thinned, and she was concentrating as if getting the cheese into perfect shreds was of utmost importance. What she was really concentrating on, though, was not looking at him. Because she was lying? Or because she wasn't?

"He was interested and you weren't?" he asked.

"Neither of us was interested. We're friends. That's all we've ever been."

"We were friends, too, but we still slept together."

Finally she laid the cheese down, pushed the bowl away and rested her arms on the counter. "Is that what you think, Russ? That we were just friends with benefits?"

He shrugged.

"I've got news for you. You took me to dinner, to movies and concerts and home to spend the weekend with your family. I slept over at your house three or four or five times a week. Half my clothes stayed at your house. In the real world, that's called dating. You know, girlfriend-boyfriend, serious relationship, maybe moving toward something permanent. I don't sleep with friends. I don't just use whoever happens to be handy until someone better comes along. I'm not that shallow or insensitive."

"And I am?"

Her only response was a shrug.

Robbie was the shallow, insensitive one. Well, half the time he was; the other half, he pretended he was. Not Russ. He'd liked Jamie a lot, but there hadn't been a chance of anything permanent between them. After six and a half months together, he'd felt the same way he had when they'd started: like friends.

"I didn't use you," he disagreed. "I didn't lie to you. I didn't mislead you. We were friends—"

"Did you sleep with all your friends?"

"Of course not."

"You let me believe that there was something between us, something special. Something *serious*. I was in a relationship, and you—" her tone turned scornful "—were just having sex."

Water boiling on the stove gave him an excuse to turn away. He stirred the sauce and reset the microwave, then added handfuls of spaghetti to the pot. Something *serious,* she said. Just last night he'd told her that he'd never dated anyone seriously until Melinda—including her—and she'd walked away.

He'd deliberately said hurtful things to her before, something he wasn't proud of, but he hadn't meant to hurt her last night. He'd simply stated the truth. He'd never felt anything for any woman compared to what he'd felt for Melinda.

And he'd never thought about what any woman besides Melinda might have felt. Had Jamie cared about him? Had she thought they had a future together? Could she have thought he loved her—or, worse, that she'd loved him?

But it hadn't been that kind of affair. They'd been *friends*. Everyone had known it, except, apparently, her.

Everyone had treated them as a unit. If they invited Jamie out, it was assumed he would go, too. It was never just him or just her, but Russ-and-Jamie. After that first weekend when he'd brought her home with him, even his mother had expected her for every visit. She'd included Jamie in holiday and birthday cele-brations. She'd even offered to let them share a room in her house.

Because she'd thought they were a couple. She'd thought Jamie was his girlfriend, maybe the one he'd marry. She had even made a few comments in that direction that he'd dismissed because everyone knew they were just friends.

With benefits.

Jeez, he really was the shallow and insen-sitive one.

"I'm sorry," he said at last. "I didn't…"

He didn't finish the statement, Jamie

noticed. That was all right. She could supply several endings. He hadn't understood the difference between her perception and their reality six years ago. He hadn't known how much she cared. Hadn't thought she was important enough to care about.

She finished shredding the cheese. After rinsing the grater, she stuck it in the dishwasher, then leaned against the counter at the end of the island, a safe distance from Russ. The air was perfumed with the scents of tomato, garlic, onion and pasta, and he looked so domestic, stirring, chopping, doctoring salad mix into an appealing display of greens and fresh veggies.

There was something amazingly sexy about a man who knew his way around a kitchen.

Opting for a change of conversation, one that might stop her from thinking about Russ and sexy, she remarked, "I'm guessing you didn't learn to cook from Melinda."

He grimaced. "She was a worse cook than you."

So he'd noticed *something* six years ago while he wasn't loving, wanting or needing her. Not even the microwave had been her friend back then. She'd lived on take-out, delivery and sweets.

"Do you ever see her?"

He cast a sidelong glance her way. "No."

"Hear from her? Hear about her?"

"No. She screwed around on me. She left me. She lied to and about me, and she took half of everything I owned. Why in hell would I want to stay in touch with her?"

Because he'd loved her. And he'd only liked Jamie. As a friend. With benefits.

Yeah, yeah, life isn't fair. Get over it.

Giving herself a mental shake, she pushed away from the counter, located silverware and took a handful of paper napkins from a wooden holder on the island, then started toward the dining table.

"We can eat out on the deck," Russ said.

Following his suggestion, she carried the

items outside instead. The deck stretched the length of the house, with doors opening into the living room, the dining room and what she presumed was Russ's bedroom. On the other side of the railing, azaleas formed a hedge, then a patch of yard led thirty feet to the banks of Holigan Creek. The furniture was wood— a table weathered silver, slat-backed chairs with thick cushions in green-and-white stripes—and a set of wind chimes hung from the eaves, tinkling softly in the breeze.

Jamie anchored the napkins under the silverware on the table, then walked to the steps. The creek marked the east edge of the yard. To the north and south, the woods formed a natural barrier. A lot of trees, heavy undergrowth, plenty of places to hide. Would Mischa alert on someone back there? Probably not. She was a city dog. She was accustomed to having people nearby.

Would Russ?

Probably, she thought with a wry smile. He

wasn't accustomed to having people nearby. At least, not at home.

She turned to look at the third set of doors. Definitely Russ's bedroom. Without walking up and pressing her face to the glass, she couldn't see much beyond the massive bed to the left of the door—dark wood, white linens, a bloodred comforter. Jamie knew that bed well. Mahogany, rice carvings on the four posters, the patina of a two-hundred-year-old finish. She'd slept in it many times, had made love in it even more.

Did Russ remember that? Was he ever haunted by the ghosts of all the "friends" who'd slept there with him? Had they understood the rules better than she? Had she been the only one foolish enough to think she mattered?

She'd been twenty-four years old and had graduated from college with honors. She'd dated a lot, had even been in love a time or two. She would have described herself as experienced. Nobody's fool. Only Russ's.

Russ came out with two plates of spaghetti

and steaming sauce, then returned for the salads. She brought the drinks and the cheese, then eyed Mischa. "You coming?"

The dog yawned, then snuggled deeper into the chair.

"Behave." With that warning, she closed the door, then sat down across from Russ, moved her fork to her plate and spread her napkin in her lap.

"Does she know the meaning of that word?" he asked dryly.

"She knows. She just doesn't care."

"You could train her."

"We've lived together three years with me the only one getting trained, and that's fine with both of us."

"You going to raise your kids like that when you have them?"

Though the question, so carelessly asked, hit a nerve deep inside her, she hid it as she sprinkled cheese over the pasta. "I don't know if I'll have kids."

"Don't you want at least a couple?"

She did, and he knew it. Four was a good number, they'd agreed. She had three sisters; he had three brothers. He'd wanted sons. She preferred a mix. She'd wanted his kids. He hadn't wanted hers, she knew now.

"Call me old-fashioned, but I need a husband to have kids. Since I don't know anyone whose genes I would be remotely interested in sharing with my children, that puts a kink in things."

"There are a lot of single guys in town. Tommy."

"Didn't work." She tasted the spaghetti. "Mmm, this is good."

His eyes narrowed and something she couldn't identify flashed through them. "You went out with Tommy?"

She wondered for a moment what it was. Curiosity? Annoyance? It couldn't have been anything more. Nothing of substance like possessiveness or jealousy. A person had to care to feel those emotions.

"Just once. I've been out with everybody

once." At least, it felt that way. Once was usually all it took to know that the chemistry wasn't there. They might be handsome, sexy, charming guys, but whatever she was looking for, they didn't have it. "What about you? Don't you date?"

"I don't have time."

"Your boss must be a real slave driver."

His gaze narrowed again and just the corners of his mouth turned up in a sarcastic impression of a smile.

She wanted to press on, to ask when his last date was, which "friend" he'd used for sex since the divorce, but because she *wanted* to know, she refused to let herself ask. Instead, she stuck with the subject of his work. "Does it bother your family that you chose construction over practicing law?"

He shrugged. "Half the law degrees in the family are used for nothing but wall decoration. Granddad was probably a little disappointed, but Mom never cared."

"All Sara wanted was for you to be happy. And your work makes you happy even if your marriage and divorce didn't."

His brows drew together in a scowl. "The marriage is over, and I'm fine with the divorce."

"Yeah. You work all the time, you live out here alone in the middle of nowhere—" she gestured to the wilderness around them with her fork "—you don't date and you do God knows what for sex. Sure, you're the textbook definition of *fine*."

"You work all the time, you live alone in the middle of town, you don't go out with anyone more than once and you do God knows what for sex. At least I have the divorce from hell as an excuse. What's yours?"

She took a bite of gooey cheese, slightly sweet sauce and perfectly cooked spaghetti, savored every flavor of it, then washed it down with cold water before simply replying, "You."

His mouth thinned, the muscles in his jaw tightening, but he didn't argue, didn't apologize.

Instead, he changed the subject. "When you left Macon, why did you come to Copper Lake?"

Easy question. She'd answered it a dozen times, asked by her parents, her sisters, her associates at the law firm, her friends. *I want to make a new start. I've always intended to go out on my own. I've got friends there. It's a great little town that can use another good attorney.* "Robbie said it would lower his long-distance bill."

"Yeah, I'm sure Robbie's phone bill was a concern."

She smiled at his dry comment. "I know you have trouble grasping the concept, but most people like to stay in touch with their friends."

"Robbie keeps in touch with every friend he ever had. He still talks to the girl who sat across the aisle from him in kindergarten, and she's lived in California for twenty years."

She believed that. "And you consider catching a glimpse of someone driving past contact enough."

"Sometimes too much," he muttered.

Jamie figured he was referring to her in the past three years, when she'd finally come to mean something to him.

"So why Copper Lake?"

"I liked what I knew of the town and the people. It was far enough from Macon that it seemed safe, but I could still get back there quickly if I needed to. It appealed to me." And it had felt *right*. The minute Robbie had made the suggestion, she'd pictured the town—the square, the lovely old buildings, the river—and herself in it, belonging. The trauma of the attack had left her feeling so out of place in Macon, in her office, at home, even in her parents' home where she'd grown up. She'd needed desperately to belong somewhere again.

"Why did you take Melinda's case? Were you that pissed off with me?"

She left her chair, going to sit on the top step that led to the grass and the creek. In the quiet evening, insects buzzed along the water's surface, and a fish occasionally popped up before splashing back and sending ripples to the banks. "I was never pissed off. I was hurt. You'd broken my heart and you didn't care. Didn't even realize it, I know now." She shook her head regretfully. "God, you were clueless. And so was I. I knew you could be dense, but I had no idea just how thickheaded you really were."

After a moment, there was a creak, then bare feet on wood. He sat down a short distance to her right, his pop in one hand, her bottled water in the other. "Don't worry about my ego," he said wryly.

"You Calloways have way more than enough of that." She accepted the water and took a long drink while eying him peripherally. His T-shirt and jeans, per usual, were snug-fitting and well-worn. The jeans had a hole in one knee and a two-inch rip in the other leg that had frayed into a mass of soft thread. He smelled of soap and shampoo and sunshine-fresh laundry detergent. He'd shaved while he was in the shower, his jaw smooth with just a tiny nick on his adam's apple. He was a brave man, putting a razor to his throat while the Queen of the Damned was in his house.

"Melinda needed a lawyer," she said at last. "I needed a client. I was new, bumming office space off Robbie, looking for some billable hours. That first year, I took every single case that came my way. I couldn't afford to be choosy. Someone was going to represent her. Someone was going to get paid for it. I figured it might as well be me. Robbie said you'd understand that it was just business."

For a time Russ stared across the yard. She couldn't tell whether he was seeing the creek or the woods beyond, or three years into the past. After a time, though, he raised his pop, took a deep swallow, then said, "Robbie says a lot of things."

"You could have hired me yourself."

He looked at her, and she could tell that the thought had never crossed his mind. He was a lawyer himself. So was his brother and half of his extended family.

After a minute, he shrugged. "Yeah, well, if I ever find myself considering getting married again, I've got dibs on you for the divorce."

The idea of him marrying another woman, falling in love with another woman, stung deep inside, but Jamie hid it behind a smile. "You've got to get out of this house and off the job sites to meet someone first."

"Nah. I prefer things the way they are."

"Don't you ever get lonely?" She expected him to brush off the question, or to make some flippant response or even turn it back on her. He didn't.

"Lonely beats miserable every time. Trust me. I know."

Chapter 6

About ten seconds after that last comment that told way more than Russ had meant to say, Mischa let herself out the door, trotted over and forced her way between them. As soon as she'd wiggled into the space, she turned her back to Jamie, put all four feet against him and pushed hard until he was against the railing.

"I don't think your dog likes me." Sitting next to Jamie and smelling her faint scents was a hell of a lot better place to be than next to Mischa, smelling her not-faint-enough dog scent and catching all-too-frequent glimpses of her bared teeth.

"Mischa loves everybody. She's just not used to having a man around."

And she wasn't making any effort to get used to it. "Does she always open the door herself?"

"Only when there's something on the other side that she wants a lot. That's one of the reasons I keep the outside doors at home locked all the time. Otherwise, she'd be letting herself out every time she saw a squirrel."

Mischa's ears pricked, and she scanned the area intently before laying her head down again.

"So she doesn't let you know when there's an intruder, but you get fair warning on every squirrel."

Jamie smiled. "It's a good thing I bought her for companionship and not protection."

She was pretty when she smiled. It brightened her whole face, made her eyes sparkle and eased the lines of tension. For just that moment, she looked as if everything was right in her world. There was no stalker, no danger, no threat to her spoiled dog or herself. She wasn't being forced to look over her shoulder or worry. She just looked pretty. Happy. As if life held promise.

How long had it been since he'd felt that way? Longer than three years. Maybe closer to six. He couldn't remember exactly when he'd realized there were problems with Melinda. The two and a half months they'd dated had been pretty damn good. Of course, he'd lived in Athens and she'd been in Charlotte, so they'd seen each other only on weekends. The first year of their marriage had been good, too. He was building their house along with his business. Money wasn't a problem; Melinda hadn't had to work. Everyone in town had accepted her as if she'd been born there. She'd shopped and lunched and shown her appreciation every night.

But gradually the appreciation diminished until it wasn't even a memory. She'd spent the money but complained about the time he spent earning it. She'd wanted more than he and Copper Lake had to offer. She was unhappy and determined to share the feeling with him.

Then somewhere along there, the affairs had started. She'd stopped loving him, and no matter how hard he'd tried, he'd stopped loving her, too. Divorce had been inevitable. Given the woman Melinda was, the nastiness of it had been inevitable, as well.

No matter who she'd hired to represent her.

"I understand Mitch's wife is pregnant."

He glanced Jamie's way, just enough to catch a blur of colors. "Yeah. He says he's living in Hormone Hell—but not when she's within striking distance."

"When is the baby due?"

"October."

"Sara must be thrilled."

"Aw, hell, yeah. She started talking about grandbabies around the time each of us graduated from college. But Mitch's first marriage ended in divorce, and so did mine, and Rick took his sweet time about getting married."

"I'm lucky," Jamie said. "My sisters have provided my parents with eleven grandchildren. The pressure's off me."

"I don't think it's supposed to work that way. Mom's response to Jessica's pregnancy was to remind the rest of us that she's not getting any younger and neither are we."

Her gaze turned on him. He could feel its heat, its weight. "Do you still want kids?"

He liked kids. When the extended family got together, he was the one who played football, baseball or soccer with them, who took them on hikes or fishing or berry-picking in the summer heat. It had always been an assumption, on his part as well as his mother's: he would grow up, get married, have kids, do the dad thing. Virtually every Calloway did it, some more successfully than others.

But did he *want* kids? Truthfully, yeah. He wanted to make Sara a grandmother several times over. Wanted to be the kind of father he'd never had, the kind Mitch would be, and Rick and eventually Robbie.

But instead of telling Jamie that, he shrugged and parroted her earlier response. "I'd need a wife to have kids, and since I don't know anyone whose genes I would be interested in sharing with my children…"

She didn't say anything to that. In fact, for a long time she did nothing but stare out into the deepening dusk, lazily scratching Mischa's belly. Occasionally her hand stilled, and the dog pawed at her until she started again, but she didn't glance his way, didn't seem to even notice that he was still there.

After a time, he crumpled his pop can and pushed himself to his feet. Mischa's head jerked around at the sudden movement, as if she'd also forgotten he was there, and a growl sounded low in her throat.

"Shh, Mischa," Jamie chided. "He didn't mean to scare you."

Oh, yeah, the mutt *looked* scared, he thought dryly as he moved to the table, gathering dishes. He cleared the table and went inside to the sink.

A moment later, Jamie came to the door. "Go on, Mischa. Go pee on something." Half a heartbeat later, she murmured, "Not that."

Russ took the necessary steps to look out the French door. Mischa had obeyed Jamie. She was standing at the top of the steps, urinating on the spot where he'd sat. He shook his head and flatly said, "I really don't think she likes me."

"I'm sorry," Jamie said, but she kind of hiccupped when she said it and then, despite her best efforts, a laugh slipped out.

And though Russ didn't find anything particularly amusing about getting pissed on figuratively if not literally, he laughed, too.

For the first time in a long time.

On Saturday morning, Jamie awoke to a dark room, Mischa's body solid and warm against her back, virtually no light seeping in around the blinds. It must be the wee hours, she thought, until she brought the numbers on the bedside clock into focus. Seven-fifteen. Then she recognized the sound of rain beating against the roof.

Slipping from the bed, she padded to the nearest window and peeked out between the slats. The sky was practically night dark, and the rain poured in a steady deluge. It overflowed the gutters, puddled in the yard and flowed along in the creek at a merry pace.

She sighed softly. She didn't mind rain as a rule, but Mischa hated to get her feet wet. The good news was that Jamie wouldn't have to hose down the deck this morning. The bad news was that she would have to force Mischa out the door to do her business, then deal with wet doggy when she came in.

Leaving the dog asleep on the bed, she went to the bathroom next door for a quick shower. She'd just put on panties and bra and was reaching for the sundress she'd hung on the back of the door when a distant voice sounded.

"James! You want to come out here?" Russ's voice sounded equal parts demand and caution.

She hastily undid the buttons, yanked the dress off the hanger and wrapped it around her, then began fastening the buttons from the bottom up as she hurried down the hall and into the living room. She picked up a low hum as soon as she turned the corner but didn't realize that it was a snarl until she saw Russ, backed into the corner where the kitchen counters met, and Mischa a few feet away, head lowered, rump in the air, tail quivering excitedly.

She was stunned. Sweet Mischa, who would expose her belly to total strangers in the hopes of getting a scratch, was bristling all over. Russ looked more annoyed than concerned, but he had the good sense to remain calm and still.

Jamie moved between them and pointed at the dog. "Mischa, *bad girl.*"

Mischa looked at her, those big brown eyes so innocent, then ended the snarl, yawned, stretched and regally walked around the island into the dining room.

"I'm so sorry," Jamie said, turning to face Russ. "She's never acted this way before. I don't know…"

He was looking at her, but he wasn't listening. And he wasn't actually looking at her face. His gaze had settled lower, on the buttons she'd forgotten the moment she'd seen Mischa. The cotton print gapped open across her breasts, and since the dress fitted snugly when done up properly, it was quite a gap. Her bra was no more revealing than a swimsuit top, but it *felt* more so. It was lingerie, not meant to be seen by just anyone.

Not that Russ was just *anyone*.

She was standing too close to him, her position dictated by Mischa's. He wasn't wearing a shirt, just faded denim shorts that rode low on his hips, and heat radiated from him. His lids were lowered, and when he swallowed, she saw the lump in his throat, felt a similar lump in her chest, spreading and tightening, making a deep breath hard to come by.

She half wished he would touch her—it had been so long since anyone had touched her, even longer since he had—and was half afraid he would. No matter that he'd broken her heart and resented her like hell since the divorce, she would dissolve in a puddle of need if he stroked so much as a fingertip along the swell of her breast or the lace of her bra.

"Do you always match your underwear to your clothes?" His voice was hoarse and raspy and made her nerves tighten.

Unable to remember what she wore, she glanced down. Her dress was a summer print, white and aqua flowers on a salmon background, her bra a shade or two darker than the aqua. "Coincidence," she replied, sounding no stronger than him.

"Hmm." Soft sound. Sexy.

Then his gaze shifted and everything about him changed. He went still, and his muscles tightened, his body radiating tension instead of heat. "Jesus, Jamie."

He'd seen the scar that sliced across the top of her right breast. It was hidden by most of her bras, but not this one, with its lower-cut cups. It was two inches long, a neat zigzag created from an ugly wound.

Flushed with heat—arousal, not embarrassment—she took a few steps back as she raised shaky hands to finish up the buttons. "You know that saying, the first cut is the deepest? The first one hurt so much that I didn't really feel the other three."

"Was that…?"

She nodded. "There was one on my throat—" she touched it, a thin line that people rarely noticed "—and the other two are on my ribs."

"You're lucky to be alive."

Smiling shakily, she went to the refrigerator to get a bottle of water. "My fortune. Your misfortune."

"Don't say that!" His voice was loud, sharp. Its unexpected anger startled Jamie and, across the room in her new favorite chair, Mischa looked up warily. "I never wanted—I'd never wish—"

Guilt flashed through her. She knew he wasn't the kind of person to wish harm to anyone. Wasn't that why she was here— because she could trust him? Because the only threat he represented was to her heart, not her life?

Now she was the one at a loss for words. "I didn't mean—" She touched his hand, wrapping her fingers around his. "I'm sorry. That was uncalled for. Sometimes it's just easier to joke."

Apology made, she squeezed his hand, then released it and would have walked away, but he didn't let go. She stared at their hands—large and small, strong and delicate, brown and callused, pale and soft. He did heavy labor with his hands every day, while she rarely did anything that posed a risk to her manicure. He could protect with those hands, could keep her safe, could make her weak, could bring her awesome satisfaction. He could hold her there or push her away, and because she really wanted to be held, she prayed he would push her away.

He didn't. His thumb stroked across the pulse on her wrist, and its beat doubled. Such a simple action for such an outrageous reaction. She thought her heart was thundering until the lights flickered around them, then went out, followed instantly by a flash of brilliant lightning. As the thunder rumbled away, she realized her heart *was* thundering. Her body had grown warm, from the tips of her still-damp hair to her bare toes, and for a moment she fancied she could feel steam rising off her in waves.

Without the kitchen lights, they stood in murky shadow. The air around them was still, undisturbed by the usual sounds like the refrigerator or the central air cycling on and off, and it felt heavy, alive with energy, awaiting the next clap of thunder, the next bolt of lightning.

Both came simultaneously, blinding, a deafening *cra-ack* as if a nearby tree had fallen victim to the strike. Involuntarily Jamie moved a step closer to Russ; his fingers tightened comfortingly around hers and pulled slightly, barely perceptibly. Then he kissed her, and when he kissed her, it was as if a storm had been unleashed inside her. Her heart pounded, her breathing became labored, her blood rushed, her nerve endings sizzled and crackled.

It was a familiar kiss—greedy, coffee-flavored, Russ—and it danced through her, its usual effects intensified by the storm, their physical isolation, her hunger and need and loneliness and old love, interrupted love. She couldn't have avoided responding to it to save her life. Couldn't have stopped herself from taking a step forward, couldn't have kept her hands from raising to his shoulders or her arms from entwining around his neck.

Couldn't have pushed him away to save her life.

Thank God for Mischa.

Whining like the baby she was, the dog wound herself around Jamie's legs, stepped between her and Russ and pushed them a few inches apart. With the next round of thunder and lightning, she increased from a whine to a pitiful whimper and started climbing her way up Jamie's body until she had no choice but to break the kiss. Satisfied that she had Jamie's attention, Mischa gave a mournful bark, dropped to the floor and trotted to the French door.

Jamie couldn't tear her gaze from Russ's face. She felt exactly the way he looked: dazed, aroused, surprised, dismayed. "I usually have to take her out on the leash when it's raining," she murmured.

"I'll take her."

"I can."

"I'll take her," he repeated. But for a moment, until Mischa barked again, he didn't move, didn't stop staring at her. After the bark, he abruptly strode to the table, picking up the leash there, hooking it to Mischa's collar, then dragging her out the door with him.

Jamie went to watch them. Russ was soaked by the time they reached the steps, his hair flat against his head, his shorts turning a darker shade of faded. Mischa looked back at her as if hoping for a reprieve, then hung her head against the torrent of rain and followed him down the steps into the waterlogged grass.

Suddenly Jamie's knees went weak and she sank into the nearest dining chair. That kiss… She'd never imagined that they might be friends again, had never in her wildest dreams fantasized that he might kiss her again. If she'd had any socks on, he would have knocked them off. As it was, her toes were still curled.

Thank God for Mischa.

She would *not* fall for Russ again. Wouldn't be his friend and occasional bed partner. Wouldn't invest her emotion and time in another one-sided relationship. Wouldn't risk her heart again without some assurance that he was risking his, too. Since the only person Russ held in lower regard than her was his ex-wife, that didn't seem likely.

No more kisses. No even thinking about sex. They could be friends, maybe, but without benefits.

A knock at the glass door startled her. She looked up to find Russ and Mischa, soaked to the skin. "Grab some towels from my bathroom," he said through the few inches of open door space, keeping the leash wrapped tightly around his hand as Mischa tried to drag him inside, "and meet us at the front door. You can dry her off on the porch."

She nodded and went through the kitchen into his bedroom, then the master bath. It was by far the best room in the house: big, with sky-lights, intricate tile work, a large Jacuzzi tub, a glassed-in shower with multiple shower-heads and a stone countertop. What a great place to get ready for work or to relax after work.

Or to set a seduction.

Grimacing, she took an armload of thick towels from the armoire that occupied most of one wall, then went to the front door. Russ and Mischa were waiting on the shelter of the porch. He dried himself with one towel while she used the others to get Mischa as dry as possible. The instant she finished, the dog gave a vigorous shake, splattering raindrops from deep inside her coat everywhere.

"About that kiss," Jamie began as she rubbed the dog with the damp towel one more time.

Russ gave her a flat stare. "What kiss?"

The one that made my hair sweat and steamed the polish right off my toe nails, she wanted to reply. But sure. If he wanted to pretend it hadn't happened, she could go along. Better than discussing it to death, right?

The power was back on when they went inside. She fed Mischa, then found a box of cereal and milk for her own breakfast while Russ changed into dry clothes. He was scowling when he returned to fix himself a cup of coffee and a toaster pastry, then settled in the other leather chair with his laptop.

When the phone rang, it seemed so out of place that it startled her. Russ didn't flinch, though, or rise from his chair to answer. Instead, after two rings the answering machine clicked on.

"Russell, it's your mother. Don't forget that dinner is at seven tonight. Rick and Amanda are on their way, so don't try to weasel out. I'm sure Robbie told you that bringing a date wouldn't displease me at all. I hear that Ginny Pearce's daughter is visiting from Montgomery. Didn't you go out with her in school? She's not married, you know, and prettier than ever. Think about her, will you? I don't expect a call back, but I do expect to see you at seven. Be careful, babe. I love you."

Jamie felt a sudden twinge of homesickness. That was exactly the kind of message her mother used to leave for her. Janine Munroe had been better informed about the available men in Macon than Jamie ever was. For thirty-five years and counting, she'd had a happy marriage and wanted the same for all four of her daughters. Since the stabbing, she didn't pressure Jamie the way she had before, but she surely wouldn't be displeased if her third daughter fell in love with someone who loved her back.

She rinsed her dishes, then went to sit on the sofa, tucking her feet beneath her. "You're not planning on weaseling out because of me, are you?"

Russ didn't even glance her way. "You can't stay here alone."

"Of course I can. No one knows I'm here.

How could I be any safer?" He didn't answer that because he had no answer. She would have gone on even if he had. "I'm thinking I shouldn't stay here at all."

That did make him look at her. Correction: scowl at her. "You're not going back to your house, not when Tommy's no closer to finding this guy."

No, she didn't want to go home and stay by herself while the mystery guy was still running around. She was a weenie, but she wasn't stupid. And she really didn't want to go to a motel. But there was one alternative they hadn't considered. "Actually, I was thinking about Robbie's condo. It's a gated community. You can't get in without the security guard clearing you. It's got an alarm system, with a panic button that sounds in the security office, and Tommy lives only two blocks away."

His expression was blank, but he didn't argue with her. He knew the River Crossing condos were secure; *he'd* built them. Robbie's fishing trip was no secret. No one would expect her to suddenly move in, and even if people did figure it out, no one would be able to get to her.

After a moment, he turned his attention back to the computer. "We'll ask Tommy later."

"I don't need Tommy's permission." She paused, then politely added, "I don't need your permission, either. I have the key to Robbie's place and the code to the alarm."

"You need a ride from me to get there."

She was about to inform him that she could manage on her own. Lys would be happy to pick her up…if her low-slung little car could handle the dirt roads with all this rain. If Jamie could manage to give her halfway decent directions, which she couldn't. Hadn't she commented to Russ that all those intersections looked the same? And he'd said something smart, like *not if you know what you're looking for.* She didn't, and neither would Lys.

Tommy would give her a ride. If she told him

where she was going. If he agreed that it was a good idea. If he gave his permission.

Maybe she could call Sara. Man, the questions that would raise. And Sara was a mother. If Russ told her it was safer for Jamie to stay where she was, Sara would believe him and refuse to help.

She was a prisoner, Jamie realized, and she didn't like the feeling.

"Maybe we could call Tommy now," she said, careful to keep her voice even.

Again, Russ didn't look up from the computer. "It's Saturday. Tommy stays out late on Friday, sleeps in late on Saturday. You wake him before eleven, he's not going to be happy, especially if he's not alone."

It was a fair bet if he wasn't alone that the woman wouldn't wake up denying whatever had happened, she thought with a scowl. Of course, sleeping with Tommy wasn't stupid or risky, unless she had a husband tucked away somewhere. Kissing Russ *was* stupid and risky and could so easily lead to stupider and riskier stuff that she would regret deeply once it was over.

Then she glanced at him. But damned if she wouldn't enjoy it tremendously before it was over.

A few minutes after eleven, Russ set the laptop aside, went to the French doors and stretched as he gazed out. The rain showed no sign of moving on; a check of the weather online had shown a system stalled over the region. The creek had risen a few inches, but was still a good foot from flooding. He'd seen it come out of its banks a few times, but he wasn't worried about it.

Jamie had finally gotten a book from the shelves, read for a while, then dozed off on the couch. The hellhound had slept, too, her snores damn near hypnotic. He'd managed to finish the bid he was submitting next week for the restoration of an antebellum home twenty miles south of Copper Lake, but if he'd stayed in that chair five minutes more, he'd have been asleep, too.

He and Jamie and the demon dog all asleep together in the same room. Six years ago he would have joined her on the couch. Better yet, he would have undone the buttons on that dress and awakened her slowly, with his mouth and his hands, and they would have moved into the bedroom for a little play before snoozing. They'd spent a lot of rainy days together in that bed. A lot of sunny ones, too. And one hell of a lot of steamy nights.

If the dog had waited just two minutes to decide she needed to go out, odds were damn good that they would have wound up there this morning. He hadn't kissed a woman, held a woman, gotten so close that he could feel the heat and softness and desire coming off her in waves, in longer than he wanted to recall. One glimpse of Jamie's breasts, one whiff of her subtle, sexy perfume, and he'd wanted, damn it, wanted sex, wanted steam, wanted *her.*

They'd always been good together, always satisfied each other.

He'd been unsatisfied for so damn long.

Her moving into Robbie's was for the best. She would be as safe there as she was here, and Russ would be safer, too. If he was ready to have sex again—and apparently he was—he could find someone else, someone he didn't have a history with. Someone he hadn't hurt before and couldn't hurt again.

His mom had mentioned her friend Ginny's daughter. Vicki Pearce had been a year behind Russ in school, a cheerleader, homecoming queen, and unofficially The Girl Most Likely To do whatever a guy wanted. He could call her, take her to dinner, make Sara happy and, unless Vicki had done a one-eighty, probably make himself happy.

While Jamie stayed alone at Robbie's.

With a glance to make sure she was still asleep, Russ went into the bedroom and called Tommy from the phone there. Tommy was awake, but just barely, and there was someone with him. Female. Husky-voiced.

Russ sat on the bed, stuffing pillows behind his back. "Hey, Jamie wants to go stay at Robbie's condo. I think it's a good idea. What about you?"

There was a moment's silence, then, "What did you do to her?"

"Nothing." *Liar.* The kiss had come out of nowhere. He hadn't been thinking about it, hadn't been wanting it. He'd just suddenly *done* it.

And she'd kissed him back. Put her arms around him. Clung to him.

"So she's been fine there for two nights, and now suddenly she wants to go stay by herself in town where it's a lot more likely her stalker can find her? And you didn't do anything?"

With his free hand, Russ rubbed the spot between his eyes where a headache was forming. "Yeah, exactly. So should I take her or make her stay here?"

Tommy was silent, no doubt weighing the options. He knew the pros of Robbie's condo, including the fact that he could get there in under two minutes in an emergency and that onsite security could do it even quicker. The biggest advantage to Russ's house—the isolation—was also its biggest disadvantage in an emergency.

"You guys aren't hitting it off, huh?"

"We're getting along fine." For a few minutes that morning, *too* fine.

"Yeah, sure. That's why she's looking to leave and you're looking to let her." Tommy didn't bother to hide his yawn. "Okay. Tell her I'll come get her this afternoon. I want to look around the condo when she goes."

Russ was about to volunteer to deliver her himself, but he cut off the offer. Tommy was the cop. This was his case, his responsibility. All Russ had owed Jamie was a safe place for a few days, and he'd given her that. No one expected more. "Call before you come," he said shortly.

"I will. Don't want to give you an excuse to shoot me."

"Man, if I were going to do that, I'd've done it years ago. Later." Russ hung up, then gazed at the phone. He could call Vicki Pearce now. She'd made clear the last time he'd seen her that she would like to spend some time with him. He hadn't been in the mood then, but things had changed. He could look her up in the phone book, or call his mother and ask for the number. Sara would be thrilled, and Vicki would enjoy dinner with the family, and if she was still The Girl Most Likely To…

He tried to imagine him and her, together in this bed, but the picture wouldn't form. He could put himself there, of course, and with a woman, but instead of Vicki's white-blond hair, this woman had brown hair that fell past her shoulders whenever she let it out of the clips and bands. She had a light dust of freckles across her nose and cheeks, eyes the color of an autumn sky and a mouth made for kissing.

And a scar marring the soft, delicate skin of her breast.

The memory was as effective on his arousal as a blast of ice water. A man had tried to kill her. *His* son had committed a crime, and he'd wanted to punish her for it by taking her life. What kind of lunatic reasoning was that?

It made about as much sense as his own behavior, he was forced to admit. It was Melinda who'd screwed him over, Melinda who'd made his life hell. Yet he'd taken his anger out on Jamie, because Melinda had left town, because Jamie had been his friend, because he'd thought she owed him better than that.

He'd dated her, slept with her, had—but denied—a serious relationship with her. He'd dropped her without a second thought when he met Melinda, had broken her heart and not had a clue, yet he'd thought she owed him because of their friendship. He was a dumb, arrogant bastard.

He wasn't going to call Vicki Pearce. Wasn't going to ask her out for the sole purpose of seducing her. Wasn't going to use her when his mind was on someone else.

He might be a slow learner, but he did eventually learn.

Returning to the kitchen, he laid out the items necessary for lunch on the island. Mischa raised her head to watch, then eased to the floor, stretched and sauntered around the island. He watched her warily, occasionally slipping a piece of sliced ham or bread to her as he assembled three fat sandwiches, buttered the outside of the bread and put them on the grill to brown.

The sandwiches were sizzling, and the dog was deciding that anyone who provided treats couldn't be all bad when Jamie stirred on the couch. The dress moved first, the bright fabric shifting with her, then her legs straightened and her arms raised in a taut stretch. Slowly she pushed herself up on one elbow, facing him over the back of the couch. Strands of hair had come free and fell over her face. She shoved them back, released the clip and shook her hair loose, then sniffed appreciatively. "Grilled bread," she said with a smile, her voice husky from sleep.

"Grilled ham, cheese, pickle, onion and olive sandwiches with spicy mustard and mayo," he corrected.

"They smell wonderful." She stood and stretched again, the movement pulling the hem of her dress almost indecently high. With her hair down and mussed, her feet bare and a soft, hazy look on her face, she looked vulnerable...and sexy as hell.

If inviting her to stay here hadn't been the worst idea in his life, letting her leave might qualify.

She retrieved the book from where it had fallen among the cushions, set it on the end table, then came into the kitchen. Without being asked, she took out plates and napkins and filled glasses with ice. He watched her pop the top on a soda can and pour it into one glass, then do the same with the second, careful not to let the fizz overflow, and he resisted the urge to comb his fingers through her hair, to smooth the out-of-place strands. To remind himself how it felt. Soft. Silky.

"What do you normally do on a Saturday?"

It took him a moment to realize she'd asked him a question and rein in his thoughts so he could answer. "Clean house if it needs it. Catch up on laundry and paperwork. Go fishing or hunting." What he didn't do was spend it with people. While a certain amount of time alone was good, too much was just pathetic. His mom had been telling him for months that he needed to get out, but he'd insisted he was good.

No need to tell Sara that he'd finally seen how right she was.

After checking the sandwiches, he took a container of potato salad from the refrigerator and set it on the island next to the plates.

Obligingly Jamie added a serving spoon and forks to the dishes.

"I clean house and do laundry, too," she volunteered. "And I run errands and buy groceries, which usually amounts to a twenty-pound bag of dog food, treats for Mischa and for me and a stack of frozen entrées. If Lys didn't provide me with doughnuts and/or pizza for breakfast most mornings, I would probably start to look like those little stiff cardboard boxes."

To keep himself from studying all the ways she *didn't* look like a stiff little cardboard box, he asked, "Why did you hire Lys?"

"She had secretarial experience, she's a paralegal, she's nice and she was willing to work for what I could pay. Why wouldn't I hire her?"

"Because she's a freak."

"Why do you and Tommy insist on calling her that? She's a nice, smart, pretty woman who's just a little…"

"Freaky."

"Different."

"Different word, same meaning." He dished up one sandwich on the first plate, two on the second, then set them aside to cool a little before he sliced them in half. "Lys has been weird for as long as I can remember. She always went out of her way to be different. She listened to weird music, read weird books, did the whole living-dead thing with her clothes and makeup."

"She was in training to work with the Queen of the Damned," Jamie pointed out.

Russ grimaced, but didn't apologize for the nickname. "She never seemed to like anyone a whole lot, and she's always had a special place in her cold heart for Calloways. I don't know if she just hates us in general or on principle, but she hates us."

After he sliced the sandwiches diagonally, he spooned potato salad onto the plate with two halves, then handed it to Jamie before scooping out his own salad.

"You Calloways make an easy target," Jamie said thoughtfully as she carried her plate and drink to the dining table. "At one time you owned the whole damn county. Your family still owns or controls probably half the businesses and four-fifths of the money in town. When you have generation after generation working their entire lives for Calloways and watching you guys prosper while they just get by, it's only natural to have some resentment."

She sat at the side of the table. He slid into the chair on the end and bumped knees with her. "You make us sound like some sort of evil land barons, getting rich off the blood, sweat and tears of the working class."

"In a world of haves and have-nots, no one would argue that the Calloways are definitely among the haves."

He scowled at her, but he wasn't really annoyed. She wasn't telling him anything he hadn't already heard or figured out on his own. "Some of us work for what we have."

"I know. And some of you never do a worthwhile thing in your lives."

"So Lys dislikes us because my great-great-great-granddaddy had some money when he came to this country and he used it to make more money."

Jamie grinned. "I don't have a clue why Lys dislikes you. Truth is, your family is a subject we tend to avoid except when it comes to Robbie."

Mention of Robbie reminded Russ of the afternoon's plans, and the muscles in his jaw tightened a notch. "I called Tommy while you were asleep. He said he'll come out and pick you up later today. He'll take you to Robbie's."

She grew serious, too. Because he'd reminded her that she had a stalker? Or was there a chance that she'd changed her mind about leaving? "Okay," she said quietly, then she smiled, but there was something strained about it. "Nice of Robbie to go out of town at just the time I need a place to stay."

"Yeah, tell him that. I'll bet he'd be happy

to extend his vacation until he's fished the ocean dry."

"Only a fool would bet against Robbie and fishing." Again with the strained smile. "And I'm no fool."

Chapter 7

It was still raining hard when Tommy arrived at Russ's house in his SUV. He parked as close to the garage as he could so Russ could load Jamie's bags without getting them too wet, then grimaced when Russ whistled and Mischa leaped in the rear door. "Aw, man, I didn't realize you had the mutt. I would've brought my department car if I'd known."

Mischa rested her front feet on the console and leaned forward to nuzzle Tommy's jaw. He rewarded her with a scratch.

Jamie stood beneath the roof overhang in the small space protected from the rain and faced Russ. "Well…thanks."

He nodded.

"I really appreciate…" She shrugged, and he nodded again. Since he had nothing to say, she bobbed her head once, too, then darted into the rain and into the dry doggy-scented SUV. "Sit, Mischa," she said absently as she fastened her seat belt, and the dog did. Russ went into the garage as Tommy started to back up. The door lowered, blocking him from sight, and she gave a small sigh.

Naturally Tommy heard it. "Is that relief or regret?"

"Mind your own business, Tommy."

"You're my case. You are my business."

"My stalker's your business."

"Every tiny little aspect of your life is my business."

"Have you learned anything?"

Tommy grinned. "Sorry, darlin'. It's the weekend. I'm off. Unless this guy does something new, I'm not gonna do anything more than maybe think about him until Monday."

Jamie fell silent, gazing out the window. For dirt, the road was in amazingly good shape after all the rain. Years of use by heavy logging trucks had compacted it until it was like rock. Mud was rare, erosion rarer.

Tommy turned on the stereo after a few minutes, and the music of Carrie Underwood accompanied them the rest of the way into town. As the turnoff for her street appeared ahead, Jamie finally spoke. "I'd like to stop at my house and pick up some clothes and my car."

"You can use Robbie's car if you need to go out. He said you know where the spare keys are."

"Robbie's 1957 Corvette? That's not going to draw attention to me, is it?" she asked drily. "I'd rather have my own car. If I got a scratch on the 'vette, he'd never forgive me."

"Nah. He'd use it as an excuse to do a whole new paint job."

"I'd rather have my car," she repeated. "I don't plan on going anywhere before Monday. I just want it available in case…" Of an emergency. "And I need clothes. I'm not wearing Robbie's."

"Yeah, sure, okay." He slowed, flipped on the signal and turned onto Walton Way.

The neighborhood seemed a little closer, a little darker, because of the rain. Sodden branches dipped lower to the ground. No one was working in the yard or walking a dog. The houses were closed up, outside lights on in the middle of the afternoon.

Jamie suppressed a shudder as Tommy pulled into her driveway.

"Will Mischa stay?" he asked.

"If you're fast enough. But I should put her in my car."

"She can ride over with me. We'll follow you to make sure no one's following you."

They left the truck and jogged through the

rain to the stoop. Inside the house, Jamie flipped the light switch, but nothing happened. "Every house on the street has power but mine," she grumbled.

"The storm probably blew the transformer that feeds this end of the street. Get your stuff. I'm gonna look around."

She went upstairs to her bedroom and hastily gathered enough clothes and shoes for three or four days. Her makeup and toiletries were already in Tommy's truck, and she had enough earrings, hair clips and scrunchies to last the whole summer. Staying alone at Robbie's, she'd have no use for the bathrobe hanging on the back of the closet door. The only other thing she wanted was her pillow. She grabbed the garment bag in one hand, the pillow in the other, and hurried downstairs.

Tommy was coming down the hall from the back of the house. "Everything looks the same as it did Thursday. No break-in, no obvious attempt."

She swallowed hard as she took a slicker from the hall closet. "If he knows I'm not staying here right now, would he come back?"

"Maybe. The idea is to let you know how easily he can gain access. Wouldn't it freak you out to know he'd been in here, touching your stuff, maybe lying in your bed, going through your clothes?"

She looked at the garment bag and shuddered again. If she thought the stalker had been in her house, she honestly didn't know if she could live there again. It was her home, her safe haven, and that was such a violation. "I'm burning the sheets on my bed and buying all new underwear. Just in case."

Tommy took the clothes, she wrapped the pillow in the slicker, and after locking up, they made a dash to their vehicles. "I'll be right behind you," he called before he opened the truck door, shoved Mischa aside, then climbed inside.

Jamie's car started on the first try. It smelled

faintly of Lys's perfume and even more faintly of the garage. She switched the wipers to high and drove at a slower-than-normal speed through the neighborhood.

Robbie's condo was on the south edge of town, between the river and the old paper mill that was the center of Copper Lake's museum complex. She turned off the main road onto a narrower, two-lane street that followed the curves of the river. Tommy had been forced to stop for oncoming traffic, so she slowed even more, her gaze shifting between the road ahead and the SUV still waiting to turn.

She hated the nerves. It was the middle of a Saturday afternoon, and she was in the middle of a completely respectable neighborhood in a safe little town. There was no reason for the fine hairs on her nape to be standing on end, no reason for her fingers to be gripping the steering wheel so tightly.

Then, suddenly, there was. The pickup came out of nowhere, screeching around a corner and appearing in Jamie's rearview mirror. The driver was traveling too fast; the wheels slipped and the truck skidded sideways before gaining traction again.

"Oh, God," Jamie whispered as the truck filled her mirror. All she could see of the driver was a shape—dark clothes, dark hair or a hat. Her hands knotted on the wheel as she rounded a curve, the pickup only inches off her bumper. There was a short straightaway, a few hundred yards, and the driver suddenly whipped into the other lane, gunned the engine and drew even with her car.

It was just some stupid kid who didn't know better than to play around on wet streets, she thought with relief. He was going to pass her, probably laughing about the scare he'd given her.

She braked, leaving him plenty of room to move back into the lane before the next curve, but he slowed, too, then abruptly jerked the wheel to the right. Metal ground against metal.

Unprepared for the move, Jamie was flung to the side before her seat belt locked, stopping her, and her hands automatically jerked the steering wheel to the right, as well.

The car bounced violently as it left the roadway. Murmuring squeaky prayers, she fought to control it, but another crashing blow from the pickup was more than she could handle. She slammed on the brakes and the car spun crazily, skidding sideways across the opposite lane, bouncing across the water-filled ditch before coming to a jarring stop.

Mud from the ditch covered her windshield. The wipers were stalled midswipe, and her head was hurting like a son of a bitch. Jamie raised one hand to her left temple, expecting to find blood, but it came away dry. She'd cracked it against the window, she guessed, but not hard enough to break the skin. Just hard enough to make even shallow breathing hurt.

Tires squealed, and for an instant, she tensed,

wondering if the pickup had returned. But through the mud, she recognized Tommy's SUV. It took her a moment to find the button to roll down the window a few inches.

"Jeez, Jamie, are you okay?"

She started to nod, but pain stopped her. "Y-yeah, I think so."

"I called it in. Stay in the car and lock the doors. I'm gonna see if I can catch this bastard."

She rolled the window up again, let her head sink back and closed her eyes, concentrating on not moving, not thinking, not being too terrified. Maybe it wasn't the stalker, wasn't connected to him in any way. Maybe it had just been a bizarre coincidence, some stupid kid playing stupid games. The stalker couldn't have followed them from her house or Tommy would have noticed him. He couldn't have known to find her on this road. She couldn't even remember the last time she'd been to Robbie's. A month ago? He couldn't have found her here.

But in her gut, she knew he had. It was no coincidence, no stupid kid. Somehow he'd known where she would be.

But only Tommy knew. And Russ. And she knew it hadn't been Tommy.

Moving her head gingerly, she straightened, then located her purse in the floor. She dug out her cell phone and the business card Russ had given her, then punched in his home number.

The answering machine picked up, the message short and to the point. "This is Russ. Leave a message."

"Hey, Russ." *Please be home, please be home.* "It's Jamie. I, uh, I just got run off Forsythe Road about a half mile south of Carolina Avenue. Tommy's gone after the guy, and I'm waiting… I think my car's totaled, b-but I'm all right. I hit my head really hard. But I think—"

There was a click, a change in the sound of the line. "Jamie? What the hell happened?"

She was so relieved to hear his voice that she felt as if she were dissolving. "I don't know.

This pickup…it just hit me. I, uh, I don't—"
She broke off, tears filling her eyes, her hands
starting to tremble. "The—the police are
coming now."

"I'm on my way." The line went dead before
she could say anything else.

Sirens wailing, first a police car, then an ambulance, pulled to the shoulder on the opposite
side of the road. The officer jumped out,
followed by the paramedics, and she fumbled
with the door lock.

The officer asked questions about the
pickup, the paramedics about her head, her
vision, her pain. They hustled her from the car
to the back of the ambulance where it was dry
and well-lit, and they gave her a blanket to
combat her shivers while they examined her.

The paramedics recommended a ride to the
emergency room, and that made her shudder
even more. She'd been in the back of an ambulance once, on an emergency run to the
hospital. The prospect raised old memories,

old fears, but she nodded meekly and let them strap her onto the gurney.

A moment later the big vehicle began moving, and she closed her eyes. The pain in her head was sharp and strong enough to make her regret having lunch a few hours ago. A sick headache, her mom used to call this kind of ache, and it did make her feel sick all over, exacerbated by her uncontrollable shaking.

The stalker had wanted to hurt her, maybe even kill her. Or, more likely, he'd wanted to remind her that she was vulnerable, wanted to toy with her and keep her scared until he made his final move. Harlan Davis had been much more straightforward about his desire to punish her. He'd decided to kill her, and he'd acted on that decision. No threats, no warning, no terrorizing.

This lunatic wanted her scared, and he'd succeeded. She was more scared than she'd ever been in her life. She wanted to find someplace safe, curl up in a ball and not come out until Tommy had caught the guy.

And the only place she could think of that was truly safe wasn't a place at all but a person.

The paramedics delivered her to the emergency room staff, who put her in a room, dressed her in a cotton gown and repeated the basic exams. She was huddled under a pile of blankets, thinking that she could survive this if she could just stop shaking, when the curtain was jerked back and Russ walked in. And just like that, the chills were gone, the shudders stopped. Just like that, she knew she was safe.

Dear God, she was in trouble.

His scowl seemed etched into his features, and his jaw was taut as he came to the side of the gurney. He took her chin in hand, his touch surprisingly gentle, and turned her face so he could see the left side. She didn't know how long it would take the bruising to appear, but it was already swollen and tender. He stared a long time, then flatly said, "You're going back to the house with me."

She nodded.

"Tommy wasn't able to catch the guy. Never even got close enough to get a tag number or any kind of description besides a small red Ford pickup, older model."

"With my car's black paint on the right side, I imagine." She breathed and found her lungs filled a little easier. "My car looked totaled."

The corner of his mouth quirked. "It didn't have any personality anyway. Now you can get a real one."

"I liked that one," she protested.

The semismile faded. "It doesn't matter. You're not going anywhere by yourself until this guy's caught."

"How are they going to catch him?" she asked. "He ran me off the road right in front of Tommy. He was riding my bumper, but I can't give you a description of him. It was raining, I was scared…"

"Tommy will figure it out."

The curtain opened again with a *whoosh,*

and the nurse returned with a doctor. Russ released Jamie and moved around the head of the bed, out of her sight. She missed his touch, missed his solid presence right beside her, but she knew he was still there. She could sense him, could *feel* him.

God, she was in *so* much trouble.

The exam room had one small window that looked out over the employee parking lot. Russ stared out a long time—while the doctor poked and questioned Jamie, while the nurse started an IV, a lab tech drew blood and Radiology took her for X rays and a CT scan. He stared, waited and wondered who the hell had done this to her.

How did you find a mystery man when you had no place to start? No idea where the flowers had come from, no way to narrow down which of the countless sales of liqueur-filled chocolates had been delivered to her, no clue who had slipped Mischa a sedative. At least the red pickup was something concrete, even if it was like looking for a needle in a haystack.

Jamie was still in Radiology when Tommy came in. His hair was wet and water dripped off his jacket. "She okay?"

"I think so. They're doing a CT scan."

"I was half a freakin' mile behind her. I got hung up in traffic turning onto Forsythe. Half a freakin' mile, and this guy came off one of the side streets and *boom*. Like he was waiting for her."

"Only you and I knew where she was going."

"I know, and I swear to God, I didn't tell anyone."

Russ believed him. Tommy was one of the few people he trusted as much as his brothers. "He must have followed her from her house."

Tommy shook his head. "I was looking, and I didn't see anybody, but maybe he saw us leave and guessed where we were heading. Maybe he knows her that well. So she can't stay at Robbie's now."

"She's going back home with me."

Rummaging through the cabinets, Tommy located a towel to dry his hair and face, then grinned. "Nothing like a little near-death experience to work out your troubles, huh?"

"We don't have any troubles."

"A few days ago, you hated her."

Russ couldn't argue that he'd resented the hell out of her. But a little time with her, a little conversation, a whole lot of thinking… "I was…"

"Acting juvenile? Hell, yeah. Me and Robbie wondered how long it would take you to realize it. He was betting on seven years or more." Tommy tossed the towel in the hamper. "Hey, you'd better call your mom and let her know you won't be there tonight."

Russ wasn't surprised that he knew about the family dinner. Hell, he wouldn't be surprised if he was invited. Tommy had eaten as many meals at their table growing up as at his own. "I don't suppose you'd call and tell her you arrested me."

"Yeah, right. Sara'd have my badge, and then you'd have to give me a job, and I'd have to work too hard. Tell her the truth. You're taking a beautiful woman home to spend the night with you. She'll be thrilled."

She would be—and double-thrilled if she knew it was Jamie and thought they'd be sharing the same bed.

There was a squeak of wheels in the hallway an instant before the curtain was pulled back. A pretty young girl maneuvered the gurney back into the room, smiled politely at Russ and more appreciatively at Tommy, then left.

Jamie was as pale as the sheet she lay on, her eyes closed, even her freckles fading out. Color was starting to appear on her left temple and at the corner of her eye, sickly shades made all the more stark by her pallor.

Tommy moved to the side of the gurney and picked up her hand. "How're you feeling?"

"Like I got run off the road and smacked my head. Is Mischa okay?"

"She's fine. She's at the station with the dispatcher, getting a lot of scratching and pizza."

"She's loving that." She smiled faintly as she opened her eyes. "Did Russ leave?"

"Nah. You know how those Calloways are. You can't get rid of 'em no matter what you do."

Russ finally moved away from the window, stepping up to the other side of the gurney. Before he could say anything, though, the tail of the curtain whipped into the air and Lys burst into the room.

"Jamie, oh my God, I just found out—" Her gaze shifted to Tommy, then to Russ, and she stabbed one unnaturally dark fingernail in his direction. "What the hell is he doing here? Did he do this to her? Why isn't he under arrest? Do you think just because you're a Calloway, you can get away—"

"Lys." Jamie raised one unsteady hand. "I'm fine. You didn't need to come out in the rain. I'll be out of here before long."

Lys's eyes, heavily rimmed with dark make-up, moved again from Russ to Tommy to Jamie. "Why didn't someone call me? I'm your emergency contact. I should have been the first person they called. Why didn't they—"

"They didn't call anyone," Jamie interrupted, her tone weary but gentle. "Tommy witnessed the accident, and I called Russ. I told the nurse not to call anyone else."

It was like watching a balloon deflate, Russ thought. Lys actually got smaller. All the bristling emotion disappeared, leaving her pale and vulnerable and hurt, and for a moment he forgot that he didn't like her, that she was freaky and hated everyone in his family for nothing more than an accident of birth. For a moment he felt sorry for her, because he knew how it felt to not be wanted.

"But, Jamie, I'm your emergency contact," she said in a thin voice. "You should have called me."

"I'm sorry." Jamie stretched out her hand,

and after a moment, Lys moved forward to take it. "I didn't think…I didn't want to worry you."

She didn't think; she'd reacted. And she'd called *him*. The action said a lot—that she trusted him, that she felt safe with him, that she'd wanted him—and it affected Russ in ways he didn't want to acknowledge.

"But why would you call *him?*" Lys pressed on. "He hates you. He says such ugly things about you. He'd probably be happy if this creep killed you. Why on earth—" Suddenly her eyes opened wide, and her jaw dropped. "Oh my God, you've been staying with him since the attack on Mischa! No one would ever think— No one would ever believe— This was your idea, wasn't it?" she demanded of Tommy.

Tommy snorted. "This doesn't concern you, Paxton."

"Doesn't concern me? She's my boss and my best friend! Of course it concerns me!"

Clasping Jamie's hand in both of hers, she insisted, "You can't go back there. Come home with me. You'll be safe there. You know you can trust me, Jamie."

"And you know I'm not going to put your life in danger, too." Gently Jamie freed her hand. "I appreciate the offer. It means more than I can say. But I couldn't bear it if something happened to you because of me."

"Don't worry about me. I can take care of myself, and I can take care of you, too. Come home with me, Jamie. You're safe with me."

"I'm safe with Russ."

"You don't know that."

"Yes. I do." Jamie spoke quietly, with such conviction, that even Lys couldn't argue.

What had he done to deserve that kind of faith? He'd treated her badly for three years. He *had* said ugly things about her. And yet she was utterly convinced that she was safe with him. It was humbling.

The silence in the cubicle was sharp, expectant. Lys drew a breath to argue further, but before she could say a word, the nurse came in. "Okay, folks, you're gonna have to take this party somewhere else because we're getting Miss Jamie ready to blow this joint. Come on now, out." She made shooing motions with both hands, and they obeyed, moving to the E.R. waiting room.

There Lys rounded on Tommy. "This is incredibly stupid even for you. Her life is in danger, and you send her to stay with *him?* How do you know he's not the one behind all these incidents? He damn near lived with her. He knew she liked those particular chocolates and those roses. She caught him putting that strip of wood behind her tire, and he just happened to be across the street the night Mischa got poisoned. Who knew she would even be out today besides him and you? And you're letting her go with him again?"

Tommy rocked back on his heels, looking as

if he had all the time in the world to debate Lys. His tone was even and bland when he said, "You're right. No one else knew she was going to be out. So how did you find out she was here?"

Lys hesitated a moment too long, her gaze darting away, then back. "It's a small town. Word gets around."

Russ looked in the direction she had and saw that they were being watched by the woman behind the check-in desk. She was about the same age as Lys, her hair fake copper-red, her clothes all black like Lys's, a stud piercing her lower lip. It gave her the look of a perpetual pout. "Still friends with Nina?"

Lys blushed. "I don't— She knows I'm Jamie's best friend. She knew I'd want to be here."

"Seems like that's violating patient confidentiality or something like that," Tommy commented. "Seems like it's probably a firing offense."

"Don't get her in trouble, please," Lys

blurted out. "There's not another person in town she would have done that for."

"There's Jamie," Tommy said with a nod, making no promises about Nina. "Russ, why don't you pull your truck up to the door? Paxton, go home. If anything comes up, Jamie will call you."

Tommy making an effort to be nice to freaky Lys. That was as good a time as any to make an exit, Russ decided. He dug his keys from his pocket as he crossed the lobby, stepped outside into the protection of the covered entrance, then dashed across the lot to the truck. The rain had kept the temperature below normal all day, and the fact that there had been so damn much of it somehow made it seem even cooler.

By the time he drove back to the entrance, Jamie was waiting with Tommy and the same pretty girl who'd returned her from Radiology. She looked small in the wheelchair. Fragile. Her face was lined with pain; her fingers tightly gripped the discharge orders and a pre-scription. If the bastard who'd done this could see her now, would he leave her alone? Would it satisfy whatever sick need drove him?

Probably not. He *was* sick. He wanted her for himself, no matter what lengths he had to go to.

Tommy helped her into the truck and gave his own instructions: an officer in a marked unit would meet them at the pharmacy, then follow them to the police station to pick up Mischa, then home. Tommy was going along for the ride, too, but he would hang back, the better to identify anyone paying undue attention to them.

"It seems so cloak-and-dagger," Jamie said with a taut smile as they finally left the parking lot.

"You do whatever it takes to stay safe."

She acknowledged him with a nod but didn't speak, and he let the silence grow until they were sitting at the pharmacy drive-through window, when he finally faced her. "Should I remember that you like orange roses?"

"Apricot," she corrected before meeting his gaze. Besides tired and achy, she looked amused, her mouth forming half a smile before thinning again. "Not really. You gave them to me for my birthday. It was just a fluke. For whatever reason, the florist had them in stock, just a dozen. You were in a hurry, and they were all ready to go, so you bought them."

He remembered giving her flowers a couple of times. Sara had said more than once—with a degree of cynicism, he now knew—that you could never go wrong with flowers or diamonds. His father had had a habit of coming home from his frequent business trips with both.

But Russ hadn't recalled the kind of flowers or the color.

Now he would remember apricot roses as long as he lived.

As they left the pharmacy, a Copper Lake police car, with the Petrovskis' son Pete behind the wheel, pulled into traffic behind them. They picked up Mischa, who bared her teeth at Russ only a couple times all the way home. There he settled Jamie on the couch, gave her water to take a pain pill, then brought in the luggage he'd carried out only four hours earlier.

"I'd feel better if I thought that mutt might alert on something besides squirrels," Tommy said quietly where he waited on the porch.

"No one ever comes out here."

"No one's ever had a reason. I know you have guns. You keeping them handy?"

"Yeah." But not as handy as he would now.

"You know, shooting a person's not the same as shooting a deer."

That was the kind of comment Rick would make if he knew what was going on, or Mitch. His brothers' influence was everywhere. "Yeah, the deer doesn't shoot back."

"It could be someone you know."

Someone he knew, someone he considered a friend, someone related to him—not far-fetched since about half the county was. He couldn't imagine anyone he knew drugging

Mischa or forcing Jamie off the road. But people could appear perfectly normal while hiding the worst of secrets.

"If the guy comes here, it's not going to be a social call," he said, glancing down the hall where Jamie was now lying on the couch. Mischa sat on the floor in front of her, and Jamie's fingers were buried in the fur between the dog's shoulders. "I've never shot at a person, and I hope to God I never do. But if I have to…" He'd been handling guns since he was a kid. He didn't carry a weapon as part of his job, like Rick, Mitch and Tommy, but he was as good a shot as any of them.

And if he had no choice, he could live with the consequences.

Tommy walked to the steps. "You know how to reach me if you need anything. Keep your eyes open." With that, he went out into the rain and, a moment later, backed out of the driveway. Another moment, and his taillights disappeared around the curve.

Everything was quiet. A line from an old movie popped into his head: *Too quiet.* But he didn't think in this case, there was such a thing as too quiet. He went inside, locked up, unzipped the .45 from the rug and laid it on the kitchen island. In his bedroom, he opened the gun safe and removed a .40, leaving it on the night stand.

Back in the living room, he stood behind the couch, looking at Jamie. She lay on her right side, her hands pressed together beneath her cheek. The left side of her face had turned an array of ugly colors, creating a pretty awful contrast to her orange-and-blue dress. Her breathing was easy, steady, and she didn't wake when he shook out the afghan from the back of the couch and laid it over her. She just gave a little sigh, snuggled closer to the back cushions of the sofa and slept on.

"Let's make a deal, Mischa," he said, drawing the dog's gaze to him. "You call Mom and explain to her why I'm weaseling out of dinner, and I'll sit here and watch Jamie."

The dog blinked, then rested her chin on the sofa cushion. She looked worried. So he and the demon dog had one thing in common.

Reluctantly he went to the phone and dialed Sara's number. As soon as she recognized his hello, she said, "Oh, no, you don't, Russell Wayne. You are not skipping dinner tonight. Your brother and sister-in-law have driven all the way from Atlanta just to see the family, and Robbie's out of town, and you think you're going to cancel? And for what? So you can sit home all alone? That's not healthy. You're a young man. You've got your whole life ahead of you. You can't just give up—"

"I'm not alone."

That stopped Sara. He could practically hear the little gears spinning in her brain as she made the huge leap from him not being alone to being with a woman to falling in love and getting married again and living happily ever after.

"Why don't you bring her with you?" she finally asked.

"That's not a good idea."

"Why? Do you think she would be uncomfortable having dinner with us? Do you think we would have a problem with her?" Her voice sharpened. "Oh, Lord, Russ, it's not Melinda, is it?"

The idea was so ridiculous that he laughed.

"Well, I'm happy I can amuse you," Sara said sarcastically, but he knew she was smiling. It became even more apparent when she went on. "I haven't heard you laugh in longer than I can remember. I've missed it."

"I know." She worried about all her sons, but she'd worried most about him. "Tell Rick and Amanda I'll catch up with them next time they're in town."

"You'll catch up with me long before that. I want to know everything."

"Mom, I haven't told you everything since I was sixteen and going out with Hailey Armstrong. You'd be shocked."

"You didn't invent sex, sweetheart," she said

drily. "You haven't done anything that hasn't been done millions of times before. If you want to try to out shock me, I'll win, hands-down. I know you prefer to think that your father and I had sex only three times, but that's far from the truth—"

"Mom, you're my mother. No talk about your sex life or mine." His gaze went automatically to Jamie. His sex life had been non-existent for so long that he'd stopped even missing it. Not true anymore. One kiss out of the blue, and he wanted more. Hurt with wanting it.

With wanting her.

Now he just had to decide if he could risk doing anything about it. Not for his own sake, but for hers. He'd hurt her once before. Damned if he wanted to do it again.

Chapter 8

Night had fallen by the time Jamie awoke. Despite the fuzziness courtesy of the pain pill, she had instant recall of the afternoon's events and shuddered, then winced at the resulting pain.

But it was okay. She was back at Russ's house. She was safe.

And hungry, she realized as she caught the scents of spices on the stove. And in dire need of a bathroom.

She pushed the afghan back and slowly sat up. The sky was dark, rain still fell, and there was no sign of Russ or Mischa. He'd probably forced her outside before she exploded.

Jamie eased to her feet, then went to the bathroom, examining her face in the mirror before taking care of business. She didn't look too scary. By Monday she should be able to cover the worst of it with makeup, and at least this time she could put a better spin on the cause: *I was in a car wreck.*

There was just no way to spin *I was attacked by an angry man with a knife* so it sounded better.

After washing her hands and brushing her teeth, she went into the bedroom next door. The bags she'd left with were neatly stacked beside the bed; the garment bag she'd picked up at her house that afternoon hung on a hook on the closet door.

She'd changed into shorts and a T-shirt and finger-combed her hair when the front door opened. A moment later the scratch of Mischa's nails tracked her progress through the foyer and the living room and into the kitchen. A quiet command—"Down, Mischa"—indicated Russ had followed her.

She was removing what was left of her makeup when he spoke again, this time from the hallway. "James?"

"Yeah." Gingerly she eased the makeup pad along the edges of the bruise as he came to the bedroom door.

"How do you feel?"

"Better." She grimaced in place of a smile. "I know. I look like hell."

"You're still beautiful. At least, on one side. On both sides soon enough. Dinner's about ready. Do you feel like eating?"

"I do." She watched him go, then shook her head. Such a careless compliment—the best kind. As if it was so obvious that saying it wasn't necessary.

When she got to the dining room, two places were set, each with a bowl of steaming pasta *fagioli* and a plate of salad. She took a bite of the soup—macaroni, ground beef, tomatoes, beans and peppers in a not-too-spicy broth—and sighed appreciatively. "Oh, that's good."

After a few more bites, she put the spoon down and gazed at him. His hair was damp from the recent trip out with Mischa, and his jaw was stubbled with a day's growth of beard. There were stress lines bracketing his eyes and mouth, and the look in his eyes was dark, troubled. Worried.

"Thank you," she said quietly. "For fixing dinner, for letting me stay here, for taking care of Mischa, for coming when I called this afternoon."

"Did you think I wouldn't?"

She thought back to that moment in the car. She had called him to prove to herself that he was home, that it hadn't been him in the red pickup, that he hadn't raced into town after she and Tommy left and found a good place to ambush her.

But there'd been more to it than that. The

instant she'd heard his voice, she'd *known* everything would be okay, that calling him was right in a way that had nothing to do with proving his innocence. He was the only person she'd wanted to call, the only one she'd wanted to see, the only one she'd needed.

"I don't know that I even thought about whether you'd go to the hospital. I just needed to hear your voice." Her cheeks flushed, but he didn't scoff or sneer at her.

In fact, he almost smiled. "If you hadn't called, I would have been pissed."

She'd needed him, and he'd needed her to need him. The knowledge filled her with warmth and eased the dull pain that throbbed in her head. Or maybe it was the food that did it, or the residual effects of the medication.

"Call Lys after dinner, will you?"

Jamie stared at him in surprise. He was asking her to call freaky Lys? Wanting her to keep Lys updated?

Her stare made him scowl. "She's worried,

and her feelings were hurt that you didn't call her this afternoon."

She was embarrassed to admit that Lys hadn't crossed her mind even once until she'd walked into Jamie's room. Lys was her best friend; she'd been there for Jamie through a lot. But it wasn't Lys she'd wanted when she was hurting and afraid. It wasn't Lys who made her feel comfortable sitting in a room with a lot of uncovered windows looking out on the night.

Oh, God, she was such a stereotypical bad friend—the kind who got a boyfriend and forgot that her girlfriends existed until he dumped her and she needed them again.

Except Russ wasn't her boyfriend. He was…she didn't know what to call him.

Maybe her future.

Maybe just another broken heart.

But if he broke her heart again, at least she would know what to expect. She was walking into it with her eyes wide-open. She wouldn't be able to blame anyone but herself.

"I'll call her," she agreed, then changed the subject. "I'm sorry you missed dinner with your brother and his wife."

He shrugged. "It's not like we never see them. They come to Copper Lake about every other weekend."

"I understand she's a college teacher." She'd heard more from Robbie about Mitch's wife than Rick's. It seemed there was some history between him and Amanda Calloway, something about a broken heart when they were teenagers. Amanda's, Jamie was pretty sure. Robbie didn't keep one woman around long enough to risk his heart.

"She is now." Russ's grin was rare, and all the more enticing for it. "When they met, she was an exotic dancer." Then, as if that might not be clear enough, he added, "A stripper."

"Your brother, the GBI agent, married a stripper."

"He did. She quit not long after they met. I never got to see her dance except at their wedding reception and she kept all her clothes on. Robbie said she was damn good."

He sounded so regretful that she laughed, then winced when it made her head throb. "So that would explain the black eye and swollen nose Robbie got last fall while in Atlanta and wouldn't talk about."

"It's a better story than yours. Though Rick wasn't trying to kill Robbie." His gaze settled on her bruises, and his jaw tightened. "I should have kept you here."

"You thought it was safe to leave. So did I. So did Tommy, and he's paid to know this stuff."

"But I knew…"

"Knew what?"

His mouth quirked, but didn't quite manage a smile. "That letting you go was a bad idea."

Her fingers tightened around her spoon as she scooped another mouthful of soup, but this time she didn't taste it. What she would give if he meant that in a different context, if he was talking about the end of their romance six years ago. But he hadn't let her go then; he'd done the leaving, and for another woman. If he had any regrets about that, they were probably just the general gee-I-could've-handled-that-better type.

She shrugged. "We thought it would be okay. Live and learn. No lasting harm done."

"Except to your car. I'll help you find a better one."

The idea that when this was over, he would still be around was an appealing one. Still, she managed a wary look. "You Calloway boys don't like anything made after 1975."

"Yeah. So?"

"Old cars need work. I don't know the difference between a carburetor and a muffler, and I don't want to add my own personal mechanic to my budget."

"There are ways to pay a mechanic that don't involve spending a dime."

Again her nerves tightened. There wasn't a hint of innuendo in his voice, and his expression was as innocent as was possible for a thirty-two-year-old man, but deep inside, she knew there was more to the words than a simple statement. Suggestion. Implication.

"Really," she said, her throat constricted. "Too bad I didn't know that before I paid the garage in Augusta three hundred and fifty dollars to fix the car that's now totaled."

"I'd've given you a deal."

"Except you were still hating me."

Abruptly he left the table, carrying his dishes to the sink and rinsing them. When he returned, he looked serious and intense and amazingly handsome. "I didn't hate you. I was pissed off. You were an easy target."

"I guess so. You, Harlan Davis, this guy…"

"I would never physically hurt you, Jamie."

She smiled faintly. "I know. I wouldn't be here if I thought otherwise."

"Lys thinks—"

"She's just concerned. If my life changes, so does hers. She likes the status quo. And she's only heard the bad stuff about you from me. She knows how much losing you hurt. She doesn't know…" Jamie broke off. *How good having you was.* But the truth was, she'd never really had him. She'd just thought she did.

But he was looking at her now as if that could change. Maybe had changed. As if they could be friends and lovers and maybe even more. *The one* for each other.

At least for a while.

She swallowed hard, then reached across the table, her fingertips grazing the back of his hand. "About that kiss this morning…"

He didn't deny it, didn't ask, *What kiss?* He just waited for her to go on.

"It was really nice."

"Nice." His brows arched. "Don't worry about my ego. I hear I have way more than enough of that."

"But it *was* nice."

"When a man kisses a woman, he doesn't want to hear that it's 'nice.' That's like saying,

'Oh, the sex was fine.' *Nice* and *fine* aren't compliments."

"This morning you wanted to pretend that it didn't even happen."

He rolled his hand over, wrapping his fingers around hers. "I knew it happened. Jeez, you think I went out in the rain with the mutt for fun? I knew I shouldn't have done it. I knew it was out of line." His voice grew huskier, more intimate. "I know it was a hell of a lot more than 'nice.' I was there, remember? I was the one you wrapped your arms around. I was the one you were kissing back. I was the one you were clinging to. Until Mischa interrupted."

Thank God for Mischa, she'd thought at the time. Right now the dog was snoozing in Russ's chair and wasn't showing the slightest inclination to get up. Thank God for that, too, because unless she was very wrong, Russ was going to kiss her again.

She wasn't wrong at all.

He stood slowly, tugging her hand, pulling her to her feet. "This can wait until you feel better," he murmured, his free hand coming close to, but not touching, her face.

"I feel fine."

Then he did touch her, just the tips of his fingers, grazing barely there across her cheek. "'Fine,' as in 'nice'?"

"'Fine' as in 'no pain.'" It was true. The medicine, the sleep, the food, the desire—whatever the reason, she was feeling no pain. Just heat. Hunger. Anticipation.

The very first time he'd kissed her, they'd known each other for two hours. Fifteen minutes later, they'd been in her bed.

The last time he'd kissed her, prior to this morning, he'd been leaving on a spring-break trip that she'd talked him into, then she'd gotten sick and been forced to cancel. Go without me, she'd encouraged him. *Have fun.*

He had. He'd met Melinda his first day in

Daytona Beach. A few hours later, he'd been in bed with her.

That goodbye kiss hadn't even been a real kiss. She'd been sick; he'd pressed his mouth to her forehead before leaving.

This promised to be one hell of a kiss.

His mouth touched her right temple, fluttered at the corner of her eye and brushed slowly across her ear, his tongue delicately touching once, twice. He kissed her cheek, her jaw, insubstantial kisses, then reached her mouth, chaste, sweet, an innocent touch. When she felt his tongue between her lips, something inside her tightened, sending tiny shivers through her at the same time her blood started pumping hotter, harder.

He didn't take her mouth, though, but left a line of damp kisses along her jaw, down her throat to the pulse that pounded there, over the thin scar that few people noticed. Her muscles were quivering, her fingers curling over the waistband of his jeans for support.

"I wish you hadn't taken off the dress," he murmured against the skin revealed by the rounded neck of her shirt.

"I'll put it back on."

"I'll take it off next time."

"Russ…" One syllable, soft sounds, all plea.

He chuckled as he straightened, his hands settling on her hips, pulling her snug against his arousal. "Jamie. What do you want?"

She managed to catch her breath long enough to say, "Surprise me."

"Yeah, like you're going to be surprised if I carry you off to bed. What do you want?"

She'd forgotten he could be playful. Forceful. Demanding. Selfish. Generous. Greedy. Gentle enough to bring tears to her eyes. Sweet enough to make her ache.

"I want you to kiss me," she replied.

"Is that all?"

"It's a start."

He quit toying with her then and brought his mouth to hers, his tongue thrusting inside.

Blindly he maneuvered her back, and blindly she let him, feeling a barstool bump her legs after three steps. She eased onto it, knees apart, and he moved between her legs, rubbing his erection against her soft heat.

So damn long. The thought echoed through Russ's head as he tried to damn near absorb everything about Jamie into himself. So long since he'd held a woman. So long since he'd wanted to. So long since the last real kiss, since the last serious touch, since he'd felt the lust and the need. So long since he'd wanted to be intimate, to make himself vulnerable, since he'd felt anything besides anger and bitterness and resentment. So damn long.

His hands were used to textures—wood, concrete, stone, brick, tools, drywall, mortar, mud—but *these* textures were all new. The silk of Jamie's hair, gliding over his fingers. The fineness of her skin. The softness of her shirt. The rougher cotton of her shorts. The warmth of her middle. The scratch of the lace on her bra. The pebbled hardness of her nipple.

She smelled of shampoo, perfume and a sweet, tempting fragrance all her own. Fresh and clean and feminine. Womanly. Sexy. The scent stirred faint memories. So did her shiver when he nipped her lower lip and her soft gasp, swallowed by his own mouth, when he slid his hands beneath the flimsy bra, his fingers finding her nipples. She liked sex, she'd told him years ago, and she particularly liked sex with *him.*

He had particularly liked it with her. He'd liked everything with her. She'd been one of his best friends. But he didn't want friendship now. He wanted to possess her, wanted her to possess him. He wanted to crawl deep inside her. To protect her. To keep her safe and close and his.

Finally he ended the kiss, but he didn't step away from the cradle of her hips. For a long time, he stared at her, and she stared back, her expression dazed, wanting, soft. Offering her an out was the hardest thing he'd done in the past few hours—though not the hardest all day. Walking into the emergency room, not knowing what he'd find; hearing her voice on the phone, shaken and tearful; walking away from that morning's kiss—those had all been harder.

"You can change your mind."

She stared back at him, then a little smile curved her mouth. "I could," she agreed. "But I'd regret it." She slid to her feet, forcing him to back away, then caught his hand and walked around the island.

He followed her into the bedroom. At the door, she let go of him and walked ahead to the bed, folding back the rumpled comforter he'd carelessly tossed on that morning. There was something about the way she moved that was so damn hot, and it was totally natural. She didn't know she was turning him on just by bending to smooth the sheets, or that he could get a hard-on—as if he didn't already have one—just by watching her walk around to the other side of the bed.

She turned, looked at him leaning against the door frame and mimicked the position against one of the bedposts. "You can change your mind, too."

He pushed away from the door and walked to her, shaking his head all the way. *Regret* didn't begin to describe how he would feel if he stopped now.

When he reached her, she straightened, pulled his T-shirt from his jeans and tugged it over his head, then dropped it to the floor. Her gaze skimmed across his chest, followed by her fingers, then her mouth, and he groaned aloud. He pulled off her shirt, careful of the bruises on her face, and she fumbled with his belt, then his zipper, finally shoving his jeans and boxers out of the way. He'd left his shoes at the front door when he'd come inside with Mischa, making it easier to kick off the last of his clothes while she removed her shorts.

He was naked, hard and hot. She wore a skimpy bra and skimpier panties and was incredibly hot. Her skin was pale gold all over, soft and smooth except for the scars—the one he'd already seen on her breast, another on her ribcage on the right, the third on the left. Lightly tracing each one with his fingertip, he wondered if she had any similar emotional scars from his own pigheaded bitterness. Wondered if he could make right all he'd done wrong.

They'd have a long time to find out.

She moved, a sinuous sensual flexing of muscles, and the bra fell away. Hooked her fingers in the elastic band of the panties and pushed them down until a little shimmy sent them to the floor as well.

And he quit wondering, quit regretting, quit thinking at all.

He laid her back on the bed and followed her down, tangling his hands in her hair, kissing her, rubbing against her, sliding between her legs and inside her with one long, easy thrust. Always good, always *home*.

For a moment, he didn't move, just savoring

the tight, familiar feel of her, remembering all the times they'd been like this before, regretting all the times they hadn't. Then her body tensed around his and she moved her hips in a teasing, torturous thrust and she kissed him, her tongue stabbing inside his mouth, and he couldn't help it. He had to move, to taste her, to fill her, to stroke in and out, long, easy, hard.

It didn't last long. After three years alone, keeping women at a distance, too lonely to admit, he didn't expect it to. The second time was much slower, at least until the end, when their skin was slick with sweat and his nerves were on fire, his muscles burning, his lungs too tight to manage a breath, his heart pounding as if it might explode.

Instead, he exploded inside her, everything going dark and roaring, and he had one moment of clear thought—*no condom*—and didn't care. Would have done it anyway if the thought had occurred to him earlier. Intended to do it again.

For a time the only sound in the room was their harsh breathing, and he could hear the thud of his heart with every beat. Gradually it slowed, and their breathing returned to normal and the sweat cooled on their skin except where their bodies were still touching. He lay on his back, one arm beneath his head—the pillows had slid off the bed—and the other holding Jamie close. Her left hand rested across his ribs, and her left leg draped over his hips.

Rain dripped outside. In the next room leather creaked as Mischa resettled in the chair, and the grandfather clock in the foyer chimed. He didn't know the time and didn't care. It had been one hell of a long day, and for the first time all day, he felt good.

For the first time in years, he felt satisfied. Any more satisfied, and it would kill him.

He looked at Jamie in the dim light, his gaze falling first on the bruises. "Are you okay?"

Eyes closed, she smiled. "I'm fine. As in

postorgasmic, holy-cats-you-curled-my-toes, fabulous, fantastic, fine. How about you?"

He rolled onto his side to face her. "You ever go someplace you've never been, or at least not in a long time, and you walk in and instantly you feel like you belong?"

She looked at him. "I felt that way about Copper Lake when I moved here."

That was how he felt—as if he'd come home. Even though he'd never left. Who ever would have believed that Satan, Queen of the Damned, the bloodsucker, could make him feel that way?

As if she'd read his thoughts, she sobered. "I'm sorry I took Melinda's case."

Two words that he hadn't even realized he wanted to hear until she'd said them. *I'm sorry.* She probably hadn't offered them earlier because he hadn't been ready to hear them.

And now he was. Funny how quickly things could change. *Nothing like a little near-death experience to work out your troubles,* Tommy had said. But, yeah, he was ready to move on.

To quit licking his wounds, to quit letting the failure of his marriage dictate the rest of his life.

He parroted back her own words. "She needed a lawyer. You needed a client. It was business."

She smiled ruefully. "That wasn't my first divorce. I knew as well as anyone that divorce isn't business. It's damn personal. I shouldn't have expected you to understand. I should have told Melinda I couldn't help her."

"I would have been pissed no matter who represented her. Well, unless it was Robbie. I would have kicked his ass and then gotten over it."

"Is that how you Calloway boys solve your problems with each other?"

"As often as not. What do you and your sisters do? Talk it out? Compromise?"

"Of course. We're mature adults."

He shifted so her left leg was over his waist and his growing erection was nudging against her curls. "Are you saying that I'm not mature?"

"You *are* a man," she pointed out, moving

against him before wrapping her fingers around his length and guiding him into place. He thrust against her, filling her despite the awkward position.

"I'm glad you noticed." He eased her onto her back, rose above her and sank into her more deeply. Completely.

She gave a soft sigh, then murmured, "So am I. Damned glad."

Jamie was a well and truly satisfied woman.

She lay in Russ's bed, the sheet tucked under her arms, only one dim lamp on, listening to his even breathing and the sound of the rain splashing in the night. She wasn't particularly tired; she just lacked the energy to move. At all. Unless he found the energy to make love one more time…

Just call me greedy, she thought with a smug smile.

Russ reached over to the nightstand, then rolled back, cordless phone in hand. "Call Lys."

She squinted at the display. "It's almost eleven o'clock."

"Will she be in bed?"

"Probably not. She's young. She doesn't need much sleep."

He snorted. "You're what? Four whole years older than her?"

"It's not the years. It's the mileage."

He quirked his brows, but she would bet he agreed with her. They'd both had three years of hard roads. Please, God, let the worst of it be behind them.

As she dialed the number, he rolled to his feet, grabbed his boxers and sauntered from the room.

Lys answered on the first ring, her tone anxious. "Jamie? Is everything okay?"

Guilt washed over her again. She should have called Lys as soon as she woke up from her pain-pill-induced nap, should have talked to her longer at the hospital, should have been a more considerate friend. Okay, so her life had gone to hell in the past few days. That was no reason to exclude her best friend.

"Everything's fine, really. I took some medicine when I got home, then slept for a while. I'm a bit battered, but I'm great."

"You mean, when you got to *his* house."

Jamie blinked a moment, then realized that she'd referred to Russ's house as *home.* In a few short days, it had come to feel that way. *He'd* come to feel that way. "You know what I mean."

There was a moment's silence, then, "I just don't understand it, Jamie. What's going on? Why are you staying with him? Why would he even let you? He's been mad as hell at you for three years, and you've avoided him for three years, and suddenly it's just all in the past? You're going to his house? You're trusting him with your life? You're acting like nothing ever happened?"

From the kitchen, Jamie heard the refrigerator closing, the water in the sink running, the clatter of after-dinner cleanup, accompanied by Russ's low voice as he talked to Mischa. No doubt, she'd roused herself as soon as he entered the kitchen. The prospect of a handout was always good to get her moving.

Jamie would rather be in there herself than having this conversation. "It's complicated, Lys. You just have to trust me. I know what I'm doing."

"Do you? Really? He could be your stalker, Jamie."

"Come on. You've known him and his family all your life. I know you're not fond of him, but honestly, can you imagine any man in the world less likely to stalk a woman than Russ Calloway?"

Lys's answer was grudgingly given. "Probably not. He's kind of cute, he has a nice body, a good business and a lot of family money. Women would have been lined up for a chance at him after the divorce if Melinda hadn't chewed him up so bad."

Jamie was surprised. That was probably the nicest thing Lys had ever said about any Calloway.

"So…" A teasing note came into Lys's voice. "With all this forced proximity, are there any sparks still smoldering?"

Though they'd confided a lot in each other over the years, Jamie didn't want to tell Lys about any of her time with Russ—talking, fixing a meal together, sharing the silence, kissing, making love. It was still so new, so intimate. "It's hard to say," she hedged.

"No, it's not. Is he still being ugly to you? Has he talked to you without calling you Satan? Has he tried to touch you or kiss you?"

Jamie was silent so long that Lys squealed. "Oh my God, Jamie, he has! Did you let him? Did you kiss him back? Was it fantastic? As good as you remembered?"

She glanced at the open doorway before replying. "Better."

"Oh my God." Lys took a long, unsteady

breath. "Okay. You know I don't like him. You know I think this is a really bad idea. But if you like him, I'll make nice. Those will be my last negative comments, I promise. Just…take it slow, Jamie. Make sure he's not just using you this time. Don't let him hurt you."

"I'll be careful." But it was already too late. If her stalker was caught the next morning and she went home, and Russ chose to have nothing more to do with her, she would be hurt. Not brokenhearted. But close.

"I don't know what I'd do without you, Lys," she said, emotion creeping into her voice.

Lys's voice sounded a little clogged, too. "Yeah, I've heard that before. You'd get along. No one's indispensable."

"You are. You're the best."

"Now you're getting mushy. Take a pain pill. Go to sleep. Alone."

"Aw, that's no fun."

"Hey, I don't want to be the only one sleeping alone. I'll see you Monday morning."

"I'll be there." After hanging up, she stood, found Russ's discarded T-shirt and pulled it on, sniffing his scent on it as she went into the kitchen. He was starting the dishwasher and straightened as she came in. He'd put on the boxers, cleaned away all the remains of dinner and given Mischa her usual three scoops of dog food. "Everything okay with Lys?"

"Yeah. She's just feeling a little…"

"Threatened?"

"Yeah." She leaned against the counter and watched as he washed his hands. "It sounds silly, but when I was a kid…Chelsea Smith and I had been best friends since fourth grade. We did everything together—took the same classes at the same school, went to the same church, worked part-time at the same store. We were inseparable until our sophomore year, when she started dating David Martin. Suddenly, all the stuff she'd been doing with me she started doing with him. She hardly had any time for me, and when she did, all she talked about was him. I hated it. I felt so left out and abandoned. I'd lost my best friend. He broke up with her our junior year, but things were never the same for us."

He dried his hands, then hung the towel on the rack. "Lys isn't a high-school sophomore."

"No, but she's young."

"So you'll still do things with her once this guy's caught, and you'll see her at work until then. Nothing has to change."

A chill danced along her spine, but she tried to ignore it. Was he saying that once she was safe again, life would go back to the way it had been before? In every way? She wanted to quash her questions, put his remark out of her head, but she knew herself too well. The uncertainty would nag at her until it drove her nuts. "What do you mean?"

He turned off the kitchen lights before glancing at her. "Lys will still be your best friend. I don't need every minute of your time. Just some of it." He picked up Mischa's leash and snapped his fingers, and the dog lumbered to her feet, stretched, then trotted to him. After hooking the leash onto her collar, he straightened, his forehead wrinkled into a frown. "Unless this—" he gestured to her, then himself "—is just a temporary thing. You know, full-service protection."

Resisting the urge to smile at the dark note that had entered his voice, she solemnly shook her head.

He held her gaze a moment, even though Mischa was pulling hard for the door, then nodded. "Grab some towels and meet us around front, will you?"

She moved to the French door to watch them—Mischa taking her steps carefully as if where she stepped could keep the rain from soaking her, Russ barefooted and in boxers coaxing her along. She waited until they had disappeared into the night to go to the bathroom, waited until she was within its privacy to give a little twirl of delight. He still wanted to see her when this was over! He wasn't going to break her heart.

Yet.

She got two towels for Mischa, one for Russ, and was waiting at the front door when they came onto the porch. She dried the dog and he dried himself, sliding out of the sodden boxers, knotting the towel around his waist.

When they were done, he gathered the towels and boxers in one hand, then slid his other arm around her. "You look tired."

She was, she realized. Despite her nap that morning. Despite her other nap that afternoon. "It's been a busy day."

"Go on to bed. I'm going to put some towels in the washer, then I'll be in."

"Mischa likes to sleep with me," she warned.

He looked at the dog, and the dog looked back, tongue hanging out, looking as innocent as a ninety-pound dog could until she pulled her lips back to show her teeth for an instant. "We'll have to negotiate that, won't we, girl?"

he said, giving Mischa a light swat as he passed her.

She raised her bushy tail and trotted after him.

Jamie made sure the door was locked, shut off the lights in the foyer, then detoured to the guest room for her pillow. Russ liked her dog. He liked *her.*

Damned if that wasn't worth having a stalker.

Chapter 9

Russ woke early Monday morning, Jamie's body warm against his, Mischa's snores soft from her bed near the glass door. For the first time in more than three years, he wasn't happy to see Monday arrive. The job had been his salvation when his marriage headed south, and it was the only thing that had kept him going through the divorce and the months after. But he hadn't even given it a thought since completing that bid on Saturday morning.

He and Jamie had stayed in all day Sunday.

Her bruises had been more vivid, and she'd had a few aches in her ribs and neck. They'd watched TV, dozed, talked, had very nice, very gentle sex.

He grinned faintly. *Nice* could be a compliment, after all.

He eased from the bed, tucking the covers around Jamie as she resettled, then closed the door behind him on the way to the kitchen. The timer on the coffeemaker cycled on as he took the milk from the refrigerator. By the time the coffee was ready, he'd fixed himself a bowl of cereal and some toast, and Mischa had started thumping her tail against the bedroom door. He let her out, gave her a piece of toast, then sat down at the island to eat. Before he'd taken two bites, the phone rang.

It was Tommy. "How's she doing?"

"She's fine." Definitely a compliment.

"What's the plan for today?"

"She's going to the office." He hadn't tried to talk her out of it when they'd discussed it the day before. She couldn't put her entire life on hold; she had clients, cases, court dates. It was important to her to maintain some semblance of normalcy. "So is Rafe, one of the guys that works for me." He had clients, too, and deadlines and meetings. He could chuck it all to become Jamie's shadow, but Rafe seemed a better choice. Russ knew he could trust him, and the mere sight of Rafe wouldn't set Lys off, while having to face Russ for eight or nine hours would probably make her homicidal.

"He gonna stick with her all day?"

"Yeah, until I pick her up this evening."

"Good. We found the red truck. It was taken from a house about five miles east of town and abandoned on a country road a couple miles south."

"So the stalker can hot-wire an engine." Russ could. So could his brothers and Tommy. But it wasn't a really common skill these days.

"No. The guy who owned it kept the keys

in it. Made it easier to find them when he wanted to go somewhere." Tommy sounded disgusted. "His name is Brent Johnson. You know him?"

"No."

"He was six or eight years behind us in school, and about all he's done since then is get high, get drunk and get laid. He has a really sweet marijuana patch growing out behind his house."

Mischa rubbed against Russ's leg, whining, and he absently slipped her the rest of the toast. "Doesn't sound like he could be the guy."

Tommy snorted. "Rolling a joint is about the extent of his planning abilities. We're looking at his friends, though. There were no finger-prints on the steering wheel or door handle, not even his. The keys were still in it when the deputy came across it just sitting at the side of the road. That's how ol' Brent found out it was gone. He hadn't even missed it. And with all the rain, there was no way to tell if another vehicle had been there waiting or if the guy had taken off on foot. Nothing but mud."

"Anything else new?"

"We're working."

That was an old Robbie-and-Tommy evasive tactic that translated to not accomplishing anything.

"Tell Jamie I'll swing by the office a couple times, just to look in on her."

"Okay. I'll see you." Russ finished his cereal, gave Mischa her breakfast, then stuck two more slices of bread into the toaster. He was buttering one piece when there was a soft rustle behind him, then a delicate hand reached past him and scooped up the toast.

"Yum, I love honey-buttered toast," Jamie murmured. She took a small bite, chewed it politely, then swallowed before offering it back to him.

"Keep it. I'll fix more." After dropping in two more slices, he finished buttering the other, then watched her fix her cereal. She'd taken to wearing one of his T-shirts both as pajamas and robe, and it made her look so girly. With her hair down and mussed, her eyes hazy from just awaking, her body still soft and warm from the covers, she could lure him back into bed with nothing more than a look, and she probably knew it, because she kept *not* giving him the look.

She slid onto the stool where Russ had sat. "What news did Tommy have?"

"What makes you think it was Tommy?"

"Someone calls to chat before six a.m.? He's the only one I know besides you who gets up that early, at least Monday through Friday. He jogs out for doughnuts and cigarettes before work."

Russ scowled at her as he brought two saucers with toast to join her. "I don't think even Robbie knows that about Tommy."

"I'm a lawyer and usually a good friend. I listen when people talk." She smiled smugly. "And though it had slipped your mind, I'm a good lover, too."

"I never forgot that." Not even when he was stupid-in-love with Melinda. He'd figured Jamie was making some other guy really happy. It was only fair, after all. But instead she'd been missing him.

What would have happened if he'd skipped that spring-break trip and stayed with her instead? If he had never met Melinda, never royally screwed up his life? Would he have made the effort to continue seeing Jamie after he'd graduated and returned home? Would he have fallen in love with her along the way?

Probably not. *Things happen when they're supposed to happen,* his mother said. Rick hadn't been ready to settle down until last year because he hadn't met Amanda. Ditto for Mitch and Jessica. And when it was Russ's and Robbie's turns, Sara fully believed it would happen. Though she wasn't averse to helping them along if she could.

After polishing off his toast and the last half of hers, he asked, "You know a guy named

Brent Johnson? Lives in the county and likes his weed a little too much?"

"The name's not familiar. Why?"

He repeated Tommy's information to her. When he finished, she shook her head. "I prefer clients who haven't voluntarily made themselves stupider than they already were and who don't pay me with drug money."

"His friends probably knew he left the keys in the pickup. Maybe one of them borrowed it, knowing he wouldn't realize it was gone."

Her expression turned serious. "Maybe."

He bumped his shoulder against hers. "You want to stay home today, we can. You call Lys, I'll call my office, and we'll go back to bed."

She looked seriously tempted for a whole five seconds, then purposefully shook her head. "I'm not going into hiding any more than I've already been. I'll be safe in the office with Lys, and with your crew across the street, and with Tommy dropping in."

"And with Rafe sitting there."

She nodded. "I don't suppose Rafe is about as tall as you, with shoulders about as broad, and about as muscular, with dark hair and a pair of jeans with a rip right underneath his truly impressive butt. Because if he is, you will have won Lys over to the dark side."

"I don't ever look at Rafe's butt, so I can't say about the jeans, but the rest of it…yeah. He's gonna have to sit all day with Lys ogling him? Poor guy."

"Lys won't ogle *all* day." Jamie slid to her feet, deliberately brushing against him and sparking little electrical shocks all over. "She has to blink sometime."

Her fingers were the last part of her to slip away from him, brushing lightly across his belly, not even coming near his arousal but affecting it just the same. She knew it, too, if that sexy smile and the sashay of her hips were anything to judge by.

Nearby Mischa was snoring again, though she hadn't been outside yet. His coffee was getting cold in its cup, and it was past time for him to be shaving and dressing and getting ready for the day.

But he was the boss. He hadn't gone to work late and unprepared even once in the past five years. If Jamie wasn't a good reason to start, such a thing didn't exist.

"Sleep a while, Mischa," he murmured as he headed around the island. "We're going back to bed."

Jamie and Russ were just approaching the edge of town when his cell phone rang. He pulled it from his pocket, flipped it open and mostly listened to the conversation, his jaw tightening. "We'll be right there," he said tersely before hanging up.

She took a breath, bracing herself. Obviously something had happened: her house vandalized, her office targeted, maybe even—*please, God, no*—Lys.

"It's not Lys," he said as if he'd heard her

prayer. "Someone did a little painting at the condo project across the river. Tommy wants us to come by."

She had seen the condos only at a distance, but knew several people who'd already bought in. They were going to be luxury places that reminded her of her last visit to Charleston, and the multihued houses on Rainbow Row.

He drove past the square, then turned right on Carolina and crossed the river. The street leading into the project wound through a grove of live oak trees, moss dangling from their branches, before passing through a gate and branching off to various buildings. Tommy's SUV, along with a police car, was parked in front of the clubhouse straight ahead, with several pickups belonging to Calloway Construction.

The first message was painted in white across the brick face of the clubhouse. It lined the walls inside in red, orange and black, dripped down the windows, sprayed across the fireplace. It was scrawled across the concrete floor and visible from the clubhouse patio on six of the seven buildings.

Stay away from her.
Stay away from her.
Stay away from her.

And just in case there was any confusion regarding who the message was for or who it was about, on the largest wall inside the common area were two photographs torn from a newspaper, Jamie's tacked to the drywall, Russ's held there by a hunting knife stuck between the eyes.

Dear God.

Jamie swayed, feeling sick, and Russ slid his arm around her waist. Tension vibrated through him as he guided her back outside, where only the one threat could be seen.

"You don't have security at your sites at night?" Tommy asked.

"Some of them. It depends on where we are on the job. Once fixtures and appliances have started going in, yeah. They tend to grow feet and walk away if we don't. And usually the site foreman and I both drive by a couple times on weekends just to check things out."

But he hadn't been able to do that this weekend because he'd been babysitting Jamie. It was probably a good thing he hadn't, because he might have surprised the stalker. That knife might have wound up in his chest instead of his photograph. Just the thought made her hug herself tightly.

"Who knows you're staying with him?" Tommy asked.

She breathed for steadiness. "You, Robbie, Lys. A number of people at the hospital saw me leaving with him Saturday and probably guessed."

"Maybe it's time for us to move you elsewhere."

"No." Russ's voice was sharp, angry. "She's staying where she is."

"This bastard's threatening you now."

"I don't give a damn. She's not going off somewhere else to keep *me* safe."

Jamie freed one hand to touch his arm. "Russ—"

He wrapped his fingers tightly around hers, but didn't look at her. "No. Absolutely not."

He looked so grim, so foreboding that she didn't argue with him. After he'd calmed down, then she would reason with him. *She* was the one this guy was after; if she was gone, he would forget Russ. She could run, she could hide on her own. She could handle that. But if Russ got hurt, if, God forbid, he died because of her, she would never survive.

Apparently, *later* seemed a better time to Tommy, too, because he abruptly changed the subject. "We know how the stalker found you Saturday. Our evidence guys were going over your car at the garage, and they found a Global Positioning System transmitter. He knew where you were from the minute you left your driveway."

That was even creepier than just being followed. What did this guy want from her that would justify the trouble and expense of high-tech stalking? "Will that help you find him?"

Tommy shook his head, then indicated Russ and himself. "We use GPSs when we go hunting. Fishermen use 'em. Hikers. Delivery services. Probably every soldier who's been to Iraq or Afghanistan has one. They're relatively cheap and easy to find."

"How did he get access to my car?" she asked numbly.

"He only needed a minute. Parked outside the office, in your driveway, in the grocery store lot… He could have done it the same night he drugged the dog, or it could have been the first thing he did, before the note or the candy. There's no way to know."

She stared at the message. At least the damage inside was minimal; the drywall hadn't yet been painted, the glass could be cleaned, and carpet or tile would cover the words on the floor. But the brick...even she knew paint was difficult to clean from brick, and there were seven threats, all in bright white against dusty-red.

One threat. Not against her, but Russ. The knife in the photograph was impossible to misinterpret. He'd tried to do the right thing by offering her a place to stay, and in return, she'd brought danger into his life.

Suddenly shuddering, she pulled free of him, went to his truck and climbed in. She was huddling there, unable to tear her gaze from the words on the wall, when he finished talking with Tommy and joined her.

For a moment, he sat motionless, his right hand clenching his keys, then he breathed loudly and stuck the key in the ignition. "It's not a big deal."

What she intended as a snort came out choked, closer to a sob. "He's *threatening* you."

"Yeah. Well. It's not gonna get him anywhere." He backed out, then accelerated, tires spinning before finding traction.

"He feels threatened by you. He knows I'm staying with you. He knows I—" *used to love you. Maybe do again. Maybe never stopped.* "I care about you. If he can't get me away from you, then he's got to get rid of you."

Russ stared ahead, his jaw clenched so tightly that he might as well have been carved from stone. "I'm not going anywhere, and neither are you." After rolling through a stop sign and onto Carolina Boulevard, he scowled at her. "Don't give me any bull about leaving me for my own good. I can take care of myself. I know the risks and I'm willing to take them. You can't win this argument, James, so don't waste your breath."

Conceding he was right—at least about wasting her breath—she fell silent, staring out the window. But on every brick storefront they passed, every expanse of glass, she saw the words again. *Stay away from her.* She saw the photograph and the knife.

He parked in the tiny lot behind the building, went inside with her and searched every corner of the office. He was standing at the window staring out when a knock sounded at the door. His muscles visibly tightened just as Jamie's own before he spun and strode into the outer office.

It was Rafe, and he was, indeed, the guy with the impressive butt. He wore jeans, a T-shirt and work boots that had seen better days. His muscles had muscles, and he carried a gym bag filled with magazines and, she surmised from the look Russ gave it, the arch of his brow and Rafe's answering nod, a weapon.

Russ introduced them, talked for a few minutes in the outer office with Rafe, then returned to Jamie's office and hugged her. "I'll check back."

The independent woman inside her—the one who thought her leaving for his own good was still the best idea—should have protested, saying, *No, it's not necessary.* The real Jamie, though, just hugged him tighter, her face hidden against his shirt, and murmured, "I appreciate it."

After holding her a moment longer, he kissed her, hard and quick, then left. Jamie walked to the doorway of the outer office, where Rafe had made himself comfortable with the latest issue of *Newsweek*. "Can I get you coffee?"

"No, thanks."

Just as well. Lys always made the coffee, and Jamie didn't feel like reading instructions just now.

She nervously crossed her arms over her chest. "I've never had a bodyguard before."

Rafe grinned. "Sure, you have. At least, for the last couple days."

"Do you do this sort of thing often?" As far as she knew, he was a carpenter or framer or something, not the kind of guy who first came to mind when you thought *protection*.

"Nah. But I spent two years in Iraq, and I was a cop in Atlanta for a while."

And now he worked in construction. No doubt, there was an interesting story behind that, but she didn't have a chance to ask as Lys swept into the office. Buds in her ears, she was singing along to a song Jamie didn't know and balancing her bag, a pizza box and a doughnut box. She made it halfway across the room without noticing Rafe, skidding to a stop when finally she did. The instant she recognized him, her face flamed red and her mouth dropped open, but no words came out.

"Lys, this is Rafe. He's going to spend the day with us."

He nodded politely, then went back to reading.

"H-hey." Lys started walking again with stuttering steps, reaching Jamie before darting another look at him, then mouthing, "Is that—?" She tilted her head toward River's Edge. When Jamie nodded, she rolled her eyes. Wow.

"How do you feel?" she asked aloud, her gaze locking on the bruises.

"I'm fine. There's been another incident, though." Going to sit behind her desk, Jamie quietly told her about the vandalism, the message and the photographs.

Lys's color paled to match her stark-white dress. "Oh my God, Jamie," she murmured. "You're not going to continue staying with Russ, are you?"

"I don't know." Hard words to say. There was no place on earth she would rather be than with Russ, but not if it meant directing the stalker's anger at him. She wanted to be safe, but even more she wanted him safe.

"Wow. I'm not even going to ask you to come to my house. No offense, I love you dearly, but I don't want this guy trashing my place or me. Maybe you should leave town for a few days."

"I thought about that." Vaguely, in the small part of her mind that had still been functioning normally on the drive over from the condos. "I don't know where I'd go. Not to Macon. Not anyplace someone might expect me to go."

Lys opened the doughnut box and took out a glazed one, then resettled in the client chair. After she'd savored the first few bites, she said, "I have an idea. My grandfather has a little place up on Lake Oconee. It's nothing fancy, but no one would ever think to look there."

"I'll think about it." She didn't need fancy. All she needed was to know that she and Russ were both safe. Then she glanced at the calendar open on her desk. "Who am I kidding? I can't leave town now. I've got appointments and hearings all this week."

"You could get someone to fill in on what's important and reschedule everything else. It's an emergency, Jamie." Lys picked another doughnut. "Trust me—the other lawyers and the judges don't want you showing up if there's a chance this crazy perv will show up, too."

She'd had to reschedule her whole life once before because of an emergency. That time she'd been in the hospital recovering from a murder attempt. Would it come to that again?

A glance into the reception area at Rafe made her feel a little braver. Not if she, Russ, Tommy and Rafe could help it.

"I'll talk to Russ," Jamie said, and she saw Lys's eyes start the slightest roll upward. "If he agrees, and Tommy does, I'll go somewhere for a few days, but I think it'd be best if none of you knows where."

"But, Jamie—" The ringing phone made Lys break off to check her watch. "Jeez, ten seconds past nine o'clock."

The second line also rang.

"Do these people *sit* on the phone?" Lys muttered, snatching up the receiver. "Jamie Munroe's office, please hold." After repeating the greeting on the second line, she fixed her frown on Jamie. "We'll finish discussing this during our break."

"You discuss. I'm going to be watching the hot guys there." Jamie pointed to River's Edge, already buzzing with activity. Before long, Russ would show up over there, and either before or after, or both if she was lucky, he'd show up here again, too.

Lys snorted. "You watch them. I'm gonna watch the hot guy sitting five feet from my desk. I'll be lucky if I even remember how to answer the phone." Taking a drink and one last doughnut, she walked to the door, singing tunelessly, "There is a God, and She likes me."

Jamie looked at the cold pizza, still untouched, then moved the box from her desk. "I hope God likes me, too," she whispered. Because if she got Russ back just to lose him by dying, she was going to be haunting someone for a long, long time.

The morning passed slowly. By lunch she had a headache and a nagging burn in her stomach. Hunger, she hoped, though nerves seemed more likely. Lys went to pick up lunch, and Jamie finished the notes on her eleven o'clock appointment. She went to the file room to pull a folder and flipped the switch, but the light didn't come on.

Scowling, she went on in, leaving the heavy door open, found the right drawer and was bent over trying to read the handwritten labels when a soft noise sounded in the outer office, followed a moment later by the faint disturbance in the air that meant the front door had been opened or closed. She didn't have another appointment until two o'clock, so she figured either Lys had been quick with lunch, Tommy was making another stop or Russ had finally found time to drop by.

"I'll be right out," she called. As she straightened, she caught a glimpse of movement, a dark flash, something swinging through the air, then pain exploded through her head. She pitched forward, trying to catch herself, but the blow had caught her already off-balance, sending her crashing into another oak cabinet.

The pain washed over her in waves; it was the last thing she remembered.

* * *

It was one of those curious moments when, like turning a switch, everything went quiet. Conversation lulled, the saws and sanders and grinders all went silent, the hammering stopped, and even traffic noise on the streets died down. It was as if the entire small area of the universe that surrounded River's Edge had been put on hold, just for an instant.

Then the scream came.

It was shrill, piercing, worthy of a Hollywood horror movie, and it raised the hairs on the back of Russ's neck. Like everyone else on the crew, he turned reflexively toward the noise, coming from the sidewalk across the street. Unlike the others, he dropped the blueprints he'd been rolling, took the steps in a leap and raced across the lawn and across the street.

People on the street were staring toward the source of the screams—*Help her, oh, God, someone please help!*—and Sophy Marchand, whose shop was in the building next door to Jamie's, was hurrying along the sidewalk, cell phone in hand.

Lys's eyes were huge, her face whiter than Russ had ever seen. Her whole body was shaking, and there was a bright smear of red across her white dress. Blood.

Dear God. Heart pounding, he gave her a shove toward Sophy and said, "Call 911. Tell 'em to get Tommy over here *now*."

"An—and an—an ambulance. T-t-two," Lys added hoarsely.

Sophy nodded, already dialing, as she wrapped one arm around Lys's waist and guided her away, murmuring softly to her.

Muscles knotted, his chest so tight he could hardly breathe, Russ skidded around the corner and into Jamie's outer office. Rafe lay motionless on the floor, as if he'd just slid out of the chair to the floor and decided to stay. There was no blood, no sign of a wound of any kind.

The scene in the file room was the opposite. A lot of blood, covering Jamie's face, matting her hair, seeping into the carpet.

"Oh, Jesus, Jamie." Russ knelt beside her, afraid to touch her, afraid he might hurt her. The wound was still bleeding, so she was alive, thank God. She just had to stay that way. "It's gonna be okay, babe. Help's coming. You're okay."

He risked picking up her hand, the skin soft and warm, and her fingers tightened fractionally around his. She made a low sound, part whimper, part moan, then went still again.

Pounding feet sounded in the corridor; a moment later a number of cops, including Tommy, rushed into the office, with the paramedics behind them. Reluctantly Russ released Jamie's hand—once again her grip tightened before going slack—and moved out of the file room.

"Get out of my crime scene," Tommy said grimly, giving him a push toward the door.

"Come on outside. I need to find out what happened from freaky Lys."

"Don't call her that," Russ said numbly as he obeyed. It felt wrong to be walking away from Jamie, but there was nothing he could do for her at the moment. But damned if it wasn't the last time he was going to be away from her in the foreseeable future.

More paramedics were working on Rafe, who looked like he was sound asleep. They'd rolled him over and there was still no sign of an injury. "What do you want to bet they find the same drug in him that was in Mischa?" Russ muttered as they skirted them, then went out the door.

There was a crowd gathered outside now. Pete Petrovski stood guard at the door, keeping them back, and another officer was directing traffic around the emergency vehicles blocking the street. Russ ignored them all, including ogling members of his own crew, and looked to the right for Lys.

She was sitting on the front steps of Sophy's shop, huddled and trembling as if she were naked in a snowstorm. The blood—*Jamie's blood*—was a stark contrast to her white dress.

As they turned up the walk, Sophy gave Lys a comforting pat on the arm, then went inside the shop.

"What the hell happened?" Tommy demanded.

Lys flinched, then raised her gaze to Russ, her dark eyes glazed over. "Is she going to be okay?"

"Yes." He had no clue how bad the wound was. He just knew that yes was the only answer he could live with. She *had* to be all right. His life depended on it.

If his answer brought Lys any comfort, it didn't show. She looked away, fixing her attention on the flashing lights of the nearest ambulance, slowly shaking her head. "She asked me to drop some papers off at the courthouse and to go to the post office, then pick up lunch from that new place across the river. But it was crowded. New places always are. And she had an appointment, and I'd already been gone about thirty minutes, so I didn't wait. I came back to see if she wanted a sandwich from Ellie's instead and I found Rafe and—and then Jamie, and there was so much blood…"

She covered her face with both hands, shudders racking her. Russ was tempted to lay his hand on her shoulder. After all, she was Jamie's best friend. They were going to have to make peace with each other for her sake if nothing else. But if he reached out, his own hand would be shaking, and he preferred to keep it under control while he could.

"Did Jamie have any appointments while you were gone?" Tommy asked.

Lys shook her head.

"Did you lock the door when you left?"

"No. We never do during office hours if either of us is there."

"Did you notice anything odd when you came back?"

"Yeah. The big, strong bodyguard lying unconscious on the floor," Lys snapped, but her irritation disappeared as quickly as it had come. "No. The lights were on, and the music was playing in Jamie's office. She always turned it off when people came in. The old guy next door had moved his car into my parking space, but he does that every time I have a closer space than him. Everything was fine. Normal."

Except that Jamie had been surprised by her stalker in her own file room. It took a certain kind of lowlife bastard to attack a woman from behind.

"Did Rafe go to lunch before you left?" Tommy asked.

"No. He hadn't left that chair except to get up and walk around the office a few times."

"Did he eat anything? Drink anything?" Russ asked.

Lys shrugged. "He brought some bottles of sports drink with him."

"I'll have 'em checked." Tommy's gaze shifted back down the street, and he gestured. "They're bringing them out. You two going to the hospital?"

"Yes." Russ and Lys answered together, then he grudgingly asked, "You want a ride?"

"No. I'll take my car." Just as grudgingly, she added, "But thanks."

It was only a couple miles to the hospital. Nagged by the same dread he'd felt Saturday magnified a hundred times, Russ grabbed the nearest parking spot, then strode across the lot and into the emergency department.

The staff kept him waiting while they examined Jamie and Rafe. Lys arrived fifteen minutes after him and claimed a spot of wall nearby. She'd changed clothes, wearing all black now, still unnaturally pale. Not only could she scream like a horror movie chick, she could pass as one of the undead in the same movie.

Minutes dragged by, too many to count, while his gaze remained locked on the doorway that separated waiting room from treatment area. If he didn't hear something soon—

"Are you going to hurt her again?"

Lys's question surprised him. She'd been so silent that he'd practically forgotten she was there. "I would never—"

"Maybe you'd never physically hurt her, but you broke her heart. Do you think that didn't hurt? She loved you. She thought you loved her back. She thought you were going to marry her, and instead you married Melinda."

She loved you. He'd been too young and stupid to appreciate that at the time. There had never been any shortage of women in his life. The women he hadn't attracted on his own had been drawn by the family fortune or the family name, and he'd been too stupid to care about that, either.

He was smarter now. He knew how hard love was to come by. He knew how rare a woman like Jamie was. He just needed the chance to show her.

"What happens between Jamie and me—" He broke off. He'd been about to say, *is between Jamie and me.* But Lys did have a legitimate interest. If Robbie announced that he was getting involved once again with the woman who'd turned him into a mean, angry and, thank God, short-term drunk when he was twenty, Russ would damn well be interested.

He settled for saying, "I'm not going to hurt her. And I'm not going to let anyone else hurt her."

Predictably, Lys didn't look convinced. "This is her second visit to the emergency room in three days."

"Yeah. It's also her last time out of my sight."

"For how long?"

"As long as it takes." He shrugged. "The rest of our lives."

Lys opened her mouth, but at that moment the door Russ had been watching so intently opened and a woman in scrubs came out and straight to him. It was Cate Calloway, doctor and cousin by marriage.

"Hey, Russ, you here with Jamie? She's gonna be fine. She's got a couple of spectacular knots on her head, a mild concussion and one hell of a headache. I wanted to admit her overnight for observation, but she says she's going home. With you. Is that right?"

"It's the only way she's leaving the hospital."

Cate gave him a curious look. "So the rumors are true. You're having a thing with the woman you used to call Satan. We gonna be welcoming her to the family soon?"

"Probably." He couldn't miss Lys's look. She might be making an effort to bury the hatchet, but as the old joke went, she would probably prefer to bury it in his head. "Can we see her?"

"Yeah, come on." Cate led the way to the door, where she typed in a code, then held it open for them. "We're waiting for a couple test results before we let her go. The nurse will give you discharge directions. You need to keep a close watch on her and get her back here if anything seems odd. And for God's sake, don't let anyone hit her in the head again. She's running out of places that aren't bruised, split open or swollen."

Jamie was in the same exam room as before, head turned to one side, eyes closed, looking even more ragged. There was a livid knot across her forehead, swabbed and sutured, and another on the back of her head, with matching sutures.

"Hey, James."

She opened her eyes and smiled just a little before it turned to a wince. "Hey," she whispered.

"Man, the lengths some people will go to to avoid Monday in the office." Gently he took her hand, then crouched beside the bed so they were on eye level. "You're okay."

"Yeah. How's Rafe?"

Russ felt guilty; he'd pretty much forgotten about Rafe. "In better shape than you. I'll ask

Cate the next time she comes by. She'd like to keep you overnight."

Jamie's fingers tightened around his. "I hate being in the hospital. I just want to go home."

"All right. We'll do that." He raised his free hand to touch the only part of her face where he was pretty sure it wouldn't hurt, stroking his fingers along her jaw. "Lys is here."

Jamie's gaze shifted to the left, but she couldn't see without turning her head. Rising, Russ released her hand, then traded places with Lys. "Are you okay?"

Lys's smile quavered. "I'm fine. The guy was gone before I got back."

"Thank God. They shaved my hair." Jamie raised one unsteady hand toward the back of her head, thought better of it and lowered it again.

"It'll grow back. Until it does, we'll buy you a big, floppy, Southern belle hat with ribbons trailing everywhere."

"Eww," Jamie responded, and they both

laughed weakly. "I'll see if I can get a Calloway Construction ball cap."

"Yeah, well, sleeping with the owner's got to be good for something."

Russ leaned against the opposite wall, watching them. Despite Jamie's claims, he'd never thought of Lys as friend material. She'd always been so weird, deliberately standing out instead of trying to fit in, and lately all her energy had been directed at persuading Jamie she was better off with her instead of Russ.

But now, the way Lys looked at her...

Tommy came in a moment later, asking Jamie questions that she had no answers for. What she did know was sketchy: she'd been in the file room, she'd heard a thud, then the front door had opened or closed. No help at all, she reluctantly admitted.

In the silence that followed, Cate returned. Rafe had been admitted; blood tests showed a powerful sedative in his system—the same sedative, as Russ had guessed, that had been given to Mischa. They would keep him until the effects had worn off.

Jamie looked troubled. "This is my fault. If he hadn't been there—"

Russ stopped her. "I was the one who asked him to stay. He was the one who agreed. The only one who bears any fault in this is the bastard who drugged him."

"You're sure he didn't eat anything while he was in the office?" Tommy directed the question to Lys, who shook her head. "And the only thing he drank was what he brought with him. So the drug was either in one of the bottles, or he was injected with it."

Russ moved to stare out the window. The bastard had just waltzed in, taken out a two-hundred-pound ex-soldier–ex-cop and tried to kill Jamie, with people all over the place, with *him* just across the street. And then he'd walked out the door, along the sidewalk to his vehicle, calm and cool, drawing no attention to himself.

Russ should have prevented it. He shouldn't have let Jamie go to work, shouldn't have counted on one guy, no matter how formidable, to protect her. When she'd talked that morning about leaving, he should have agreed, should have taken her out of town himself.

He should have done a better job watching over her.

Finally Cate laid the chart aside. "Well, Jamie, if you're sure you don't want to spend the night with us, we'll get rid of these guys and get you dressed and out of here."

"I'm sure."

Russ squeezed her hand as he followed Tommy out the door and back down to the waiting room. Looking more serious than usual, Tommy went to a deserted spot, then faced him. "I didn't want to say anything to Jamie just yet, but there was another note. He left it on her desk."

Russ had glanced at her desk only long enough to see that she wasn't sitting there. He had a vague memory of papers and files, nothing more. "What did it say?"

"'Get rid of him.'"

Stay away from her. Get rid of him. "Bossy bastard, isn't he?" he asked with a grim smile.

After a moment, they both spoke at the same time. "About my suggestion— Maybe moving her—"

Tommy broke off, and Russ went on. "Maybe moving her is a good idea."

"Where would you go?"

Russ shrugged. Between them, his aunts and uncles had probably a dozen vacation homes, from the Georgia coast to Vail. Any of them would be happy to give him the keys for a while. Or they could go to some touristy place and rent a cottage under a fake name, or move from motel to motel, or take a road trip. They could get lost in a city, the bigger, the better.

"I'll figure something out. Right now—" His gaze moved to the security door as it opened. A kid in scrubs pushed Jamie through in a wheelchair. Lys was behind them, clutching a handful of papers. "She's in no shape to travel." She was pale, slumped in the chair, one hand pressed to her right temple as if trying to ease an ache there.

Tommy turned to look, too. "Yeah. If he keeps cracking her skull, the son of a bitch's going to kill her whether he means to or not. I wish I could assign a couple guys to watch her."

But he couldn't. Private security wasn't the police department's job. Jamie's private security was Russ's job.

"I'll get someone." And he was going to move her. She might be too weak for a long journey, but the place he had in mind was only a mile or so south of his house. It had never been part of Granddad's logging operation, so there was only the one road in.

And he wasn't telling anyone, not even Tommy.

Damned if he was going to let anything happen to her again.

Chapter 10

On the unending ride home, Jamie's head throbbed, a bruise formed on her shoulder, and the acid in her stomach had reached boiling point. She wanted bed and food in that order, so it was with relief that she recognized the last crossroad before reaching Russ's house.

He'd been on the cell phone for a while, but she felt so crappy that she hadn't even listened. Now, as they rounded the last curve and the house came into sight, she roused herself to summon the energy to walk inside and to the bedroom.

Russ had different plans. He laid his hand over hers when she started to unfasten the seat belt. "We're not staying here. I just came to get some clothes and Mischa."

The idea of sitting upright for even another mile was enough to make her head throb in new places. "Where are we going?"

"Rick's house. It's not far. Wait here and I'll get what we need."

She was so woozy that she knew she'd lost track of time. It seemed only a moment before he returned with suitcases that he put in the back, a moment after that with two handfuls of plastic sacks filled with groceries, once more with Mischa and her dog food.

The dog jumped into the truck, sniffed curiously around Jamie, then sat down and gently nuzzled her. Jamie wrapped her arm around her; that was the extent of her energy.

Back over the hard-packed road, onto the highway heading into town, then onto another dirt road. This one was less traveled, bumpier, and it increased her discomfort to the point that she thought she might cry, when she *never* cried from physical pain. Not when she'd been stabbed, not when she'd been run off the road. Her tears were saved for emotional pain, like getting her heart broken.

Or, she added with a glance at Russ, getting it put back together.

Finally, they reached Holigan Creek and the house that, like Russ's, sat on the bank. It was a log cabin, smaller than his, but charming just the same. It faced south, with a wraparound porch that offered views of the creek to the east. He pulled into the garage, shut off the engine and waited until the door was closed again before he got out.

He helped her inside, through a large family room-kitchen with sleeping space in a loft overhead, past a guest room and into the master suite. She barely noticed the colors—burnished yellow, khaki and rust—as he settled her on the bed.

"Crackers?"

She nodded once and regretted it.

He made several trips back to the garage, and before long, she was stripped down to her panties, wearing one of his T-shirts and munching from a sleeve of saltine crackers, feeling marginally better.

Russ put away the groceries, their clothes and toiletries, then fixed a couple of ham sandwiches and brought them, with water and chips, into the bedroom. She made room for him to sit beside her, then took a cautious bite of her sandwich. "You're very good at pampering."

He grinned. "I expect the same next time I get thumped on the head."

"There's been a first time?"

"Hell, yeah. Rick and Robbie have probably done it twelve or fifteen times, and one time at work, I fell off a scaffolding and pitched head-first onto a stack of drywall. Broke the top sheet of the drywall. Just gave me a bit of a headache."

She smiled faintly, then it faded. "What did Tommy tell you when you went out to the waiting room with him?"

His gaze steady, he told her about the note. It was ominous enough on its own, but the implied threat—*or I will*—made her blood run cold. "Lys's grandfather has a place at Lake Oconee."

She expected an argument, but it didn't come. "My family's got places all over. Or we could just see the U.S.A. in my Chevrolet. But first you need some time to rest."

"You don't have to go with me."

"Yes, I do."

Her smile was thin and regretful. "Because he's targeting you now."

Russ finished off his sandwich, then picked up the other half of hers. "He's not getting to you again unless he kills me first."

"I don't want your death on my conscience."

He studied her while he chewed, then drained half his water in one swallow. His grin came back slowly, broad and sexy enough to stir a tingle of desire deep inside her. "I've got plans for you and me, James, and they don't include dying an untimely death."

"What—" She cleared her throat, but her voice was still husky. "What kind of plans?"

"Long-term."

"Friends with benefits?"

"Friends, I hope. It's no fun living with someone you don't like. But more than that."

She ate a little of her sandwich while considering that. The warmth in his voice and his gaze was going a long way to ease her discomfort. "I hope, too," she murmured before taking another bite.

She dozed off and on through the afternoon and into the evening. Sometimes when she awoke, Russ was sitting in a chair nearby, reading or staring out the window or just watching her. Once she caught a glimpse of him outside, tossing a chewed-up tennis ball for Mischa to fetch. A couple of times he was on his cell phone in the next room, his voice a distant rumble, familiar, comforting.

The glowing numbers on the nightstand clock showed 10:43 p.m. when she finally got up and went into the connecting bathroom before padding into the kitchen for what she needed next: a cold drink and Russ.

He was standing at the long peninsula that separated the kitchen from the family room, staring fixedly into the distance, looking worried. Lord knew, she came with plenty of things to trouble him. Her stalker. The vandalism to his job site. The threat against him. The ongoing upheaval in his life.

He didn't notice her until she slid onto a stool opposite him. "Hey," she said softly.

His gaze moved over her, pausing on her forehead. Even if a look in the bathroom mirror hadn't told her that she looked pretty bad, she would guess it from the way his eyes narrowed and his jaw tightened. Anger entered his expression, followed by determination and something else, something softer, warmer, sweeter. It made her blood hot and her knees weak, and instantly everything felt better.

He gestured toward the cooktop beside him. "How about some soup?"

She sniffed the redolent air, decided she was hungry and nodded. As if glad of something to do, he filled a bowl from the pot, got silverware, a glass of ice and a bottle of water and opened a new sleeve of crackers, then set everything in front of her. Standing back, arms folded across his chest, he leaned against the counter and watched until she'd finished all but a few bites of the soup.

"What's on your mind?" she asked as she pushed the bowl a few inches away.

"You. What happened."

"Have you heard anything about Rafe?"

"He's awake. Fine. Pissed he let his guard down."

"It wasn't his fault."

"No," Russ agreed. Once again he busied

himself, rinsing the bowl, putting away the crackers, storing the leftover soup in the refrigerator. She didn't offer her help, aware he wouldn't accept it and, truly, not sure how much help she could be. Her head was still hurting, and just about every expression she made, she'd discovered, tugged on the stitches across her forehead.

"Hey, James." His back was to her, his voice muffled. "When did you start eating Mexican food?"

Curious question, even more curious tone. Too casual. She tried to sound just casual. "I don't eat Mexican. Not since I was ten and threw up in the middle of La Cantina at my sister's birthday party. Considering the number of times you tried to get me to eat it in school, and the number of times I refused, I'd think you'd remember."

Though there was a lot he hadn't remembered about the two of them together, because he hadn't been serious about her. In the past few days that knowledge had lost most of its power. Only a faint twinge of regret stirred inside her.

"I do remember. I was just so damn worried about you that it took a while..." He faced her then, lines of tension marking the corners of his mouth, looking as if what he had to say was unpleasant. "Lys told Tommy and me that she was gone to get lunch when you were attacked. She said you wanted it from the new restaurant across the river."

Jamie thought back to that morning. The doctor had told her not to worry if her memory of the events just before the assault was fuzzy or missing altogether. It was common in a head injury, and since she'd gotten conked twice that day—once by her assailant, once when she fell—and was already concussed from the car accident, it was even expected in her case. "I don't remember. I might have."

"The condos are just one of our projects on the west side. We've got four houses going up in the new subdivision downriver, so I spend a lot of time over there. There's not much commercial development yet—a couple convenience stores, a movie rental place, a fast-food drive-through…and the new restaurant. Taquito Tacos."

Maybe it was all the knocks to the head she'd taken; maybe it was stress or fuzziness from sleeping most of the afternoon and evening, but it took a moment for his words to sink in. When they did, she felt a moment's queasiness, as if dinner might reappear.

"She said you *asked* for Mexican food for lunch. Why would she say that?"

"She must have misunderstood. Or maybe she asked if I wanted to try the new place, thinking I knew what it was, and not knowing, I said yes." Both were plausible excuses. Except for the fact that Lys rarely got anything wrong, and while Jamie could clearly remember asking her to go to the post office and the courthouse and to pick up lunch while she was out, she couldn't for the life of her recall a discussion of where to get the food. She often left the choice to Lys, who knew her favorites at every restaurant in town.

"Have you ever told her you don't like Mexican food?" Russ asked quietly.

Jamie wished she could give the same answer as before: *I don't remember.* But she did. Lys had been aghast at the idea of anyone who didn't find great pleasure in queso, salsa, fajitas and carne asada. She'd even tried to entice Jamie to Tia Maria's with the promise of the best margaritas in three counties.

"Yes," she said softly, hating the answer, hating what she was thinking, what he was clearly thinking. "Maybe…maybe she…" She was such a bad friend because she couldn't come up with a single excuse that wasn't flimsy. There was only one reason for Lys to lie: she didn't want anyone to know where she'd been or what she'd done. Why? What was she hiding? Was she somehow involved with Jamie's stalker? Was she protecting him or—Jamie felt crappy for even thinking it—helping him?

She shied away from the idea. Lys was her best friend. She would never help anyone who threatened Jamie. *Never.* The idea was too ridiculous to consider.

"There's got to be some explanation," she said, her face warming while her core turned cold.

"Like what? She confused you with her other best friend?"

He didn't have to spell it out: Lys's life wasn't exactly overflowing with friends. In fact, outside of the occasional date or family events, her social life was pretty much time spent with Jamie.

Russ pressed on. "Does she know you like those roses?"

Again, she wished she could say *I don't remember.* Again, she couldn't. "She—she's ordered them online for me a couple times."

"And the chocolates?"

She nodded bleakly.

"She had access to your car. She was there the night you should have gotten a flat. She knows Mischa and would have no trouble feeding her something laced with sedatives. She knows our history and knows that we're back together. She feels threatened by me. You said so yourself."

"Yes, but…she's my *friend*. She can't be a stalker. My stalker is supposed to be a guy." She knew it was a silly thing to say. Stalkers came in all types. But it was more common for men to stalk women, or vice versa, than for a woman to stalk another woman. That just added a little extra to the creep factor.

"All a stalker has to be is obsessed."

"And you think Lys is obsessed with me?"

He rested his elbows on the counter, bringing him much closer. "Today at the hospital, when you were talking to her, the way she looked at you…I knew that look, but I didn't recognize it, then Tommy came in, and Cate. It wasn't until I was watching you sleep a while ago that I knew. She was looking at you the way I do. Like…like she's in love with you."

Jamie stilled in the act of reaching for her glass, her hand utterly motionless. Had he just said that he was in love with her? She wanted to ask him to repeat it in a more straightforward fashion, wanted to tell him that she loved him again, too, that maybe deep inside she'd never stopped. But he looked so damn grim and this wasn't exactly the conversation where she wanted to lay bare her most tender feelings.

"Of course she loves me," she said in a halfhearted protest. "She's my best friend. Best friends love each other."

"Not love, James. *In* love. You know the difference as well as I do."

"But…she's not…I'm not…I'd never…" Jamie stared at the counter. Other people could have known about the flowers and the chocolates; though Lys didn't have many friends, Jamie did. And anyone could have planted the GPS on her car; it sat outside her office all day and her house all night. And Mischa was a friendly dog; the only person she'd ever disliked on meeting was Russ, and she'd changed her mind about him soon enough. Offer her food, and she would be your new best buddy.

But who besides Lys had known that Jamie would go back to the office after her trip to Augusta last Wednesday? Who had known that nothing-special rental car had taken the place of her convertible? Who had come around the corner mere moments after Jamie's tire would have gone flat, if Russ hadn't interfered? Lys had said she'd gone to pick up a pizza—the woman who had Luigi's on speed dial for delivery.

Who had known today that Rafe would remain in the office with Jamie when Lys went out? What were the odds that the stalker had coincidentally come prepared for a second victim even though he'd waited until the only other person usually in the office was gone?

Her shoulders sagging, Jamie covered her face with her hands, winced and lowered them again. "I tell her I love her, that I don't know what I'd do without her, that meeting her was my lucky day, but I mean it as a *friend.* Why would she think…?"

"She's not thinking. She's obsessing."

"But she dates guys!"

"And she's in love with you."

Jamie shivered, and Russ came around the end of the counter to gather her into his arms. She leaned against him, absorbing his warmth, his strength, wishing he could somehow make this whole mess go away.

But it was this mess that had brought them back together.

She clung to him a while before finally murmuring, "We should tell Tommy."

"Yeah." But Russ made no move to release her.

"If we're wrong, she'll be so hurt that I suspected her."

"We'll find a way to apologize."

After a few minutes, he let go, picked up his cell phone from the coffee table and came back to stand beside her. She could hear the faint ringing, then Tommy's voice, pretty alert considering the hour. She couldn't make out his words, and Russ's responses were terse, offering no information: *Good. Really? Yeah.*

Then the meat: "That's not the only thing she lied about." He repeated his and Jamie's suspicions, while she clung to the fading hope that it was all just a horrible misunderstanding. How could she have been so wrong about Lys? How could she have become friends with a woman who could do the things Lys had apparently done? Why hadn't she known?

Finally Russ hung up. Instead of relating the conversation to her immediately, he slid the phone into his pocket, then picked up Jamie.

"I can walk," she said, her protest too feeble

by far. She liked being in his arms. She'd never felt safer.

As they passed through the family room, he gave a short whistle and Mischa, stretched out on the couch, jumped to her feet and followed them into the bedroom. He settled Jamie in bed, folded the comforter in fourths, tossed it into a corner for Mischa, then stripped off his clothes and joined her. He laid his cell phone on the night table, next to one of his pistols, and gathered her into his arms.

"Rafe's been awake off and on this evening, but kind of woozy. He's finally clearheaded enough for Tommy to question him."

Jamie knew from his tone that she wasn't going to like what he had to say. She wanted to stick her fingers in her ears, clap her hands over his mouth or kiss him into silence, but she remained stiff and still and waited.

"Lys told us that Rafe hadn't eaten or drunk anything except the stuff he brought with him. She *didn't* tell us that she got him a cup of ice before she left on her errands. He poured the bottled stuff into it, drank it, and the next thing he knew, he was waking up in the hospital. And when the evidence guys searched the office, they didn't find the cup."

Her heart sank.

"You said you heard a thud in the outer office, then the door opening or closing. Tommy thinks Lys was hanging out in the hall, waiting for the drug to take effect. When Rafe fell from the chair, she came in and—and attacked you." His muscles tightened with the last words, and he wrapped his arm a little tighter around her.

"So she hit me, left the note on my desk and got rid of the cup she'd given Rafe. Then she came back and 'found' me, got a bit of my blood on her for effect and ran out screaming."

"Yeah. And remember Brent Johnson? The guy who owned the truck that ran you off the road? Tommy's been checking him out. Three guesses who he used to date."

Guilt was giving way to anger. Maybe she was finding it too easy to place blame on Lys; maybe a true friend would insist on proof. But a true friend wouldn't poison her dog. A true friend wouldn't terrorize her, wouldn't try to hurt her, maybe even kill her. A true friend wouldn't threaten the man she loved or the stranger who was doing nothing but keeping an eye on her.

But Jamie had *always* believed Lys was a true friend. She'd always trusted her, had faith in her. And *this* was what she'd gotten in return.

"Is Tommy going to question her?" she asked, her voice small and quiet.

"He was on his way there when we hung up."

As if on cue, the cell phone rang and Russ grabbed it. It was a short conversation, and he ended it looking even grimmer. "She's not home. They're checking for her car around town."

"Should we go someplace else?"

"No. I've got guys watching the road and the house, people who work security for the family. We're okay here for the night."

For the night. That was all they could hope for right now—to survive the night. And then they would get through tomorrow and tomorrow night, and sooner or later, Tommy would find Lys.

Sooner or later, this nightmare would be over.

Ordinarily Russ was out of bed before sunrise, ready to get to work and face the day, but the previous day had been far from ordinary. Though he and Jamie had stopped talking after he'd reassured her that they were safe, neither of them had fallen asleep for a long time. Once he'd drifted off, he hadn't changed position, and his body was protesting.

Jamie was using his left arm for a pillow, so he raised his right hand to his face, rubbing his eyes, then scratching across the bristle on his jaw. He looked at her, at the dark sutures and the rainbow of colors that marked half her face, and everything in him stiffened all over again. The desire to shake Lys like a junkyard dog with a rag doll clenched his free fingers into a fist before he pushed it to the back of his mind.

He glanced around, needing a moment to realize he wasn't in his bed, another moment to remember where he was. The clock said 5:25 a.m. Everything was quiet, Jamie's breathing slow and soft, Mischa's deep and rumbling. He wasn't sure if he'd just awakened, or if something had disturbed his sleep.

Then he heard it—a discordant hum coming from somewhere on the floor. He eased away from Jamie and slid out of bed, then located her purse where he'd dropped it the day before. The hum stopped, then started again within seconds. He turned back the flap that closed the purse and located her cell phone inside, set to vibrate instead of ring. The screen showed a number, no name. He flipped it open on his way out of the bedroom and said hello.

"Russ, it's Lys. I need to talk to Jamie right away!"

The anger returned, but he kept it tautly under control. "She's asleep, and I don't want to wake her."

"But it's an emergency!"

"Tell me."

There was silence for a moment, broken by the sound of a car passing at her end. "Okay. I guess… Yeah. I mean, you two are together, right?"

"Right," he agreed with more force than was necessary. He'd already told her at the hospital that he was going to watch out for Jamie for the rest of their lives. That had probably goaded her into whatever plan she was putting in motion now.

Probably a plan to get him out of her way.

"Okay. I went out for my usual run this morning, and when I came by the office, I glanced in the window, and—" Her voice began trembling. From fear, he would have guessed twenty-four hours ago. Excitement, he knew now. "Everything's been trashed—the files, the furniture, the pictures on the wall. It's a mess. She's got to get down here. All of our clients' confidential records…"

After the past eighteen hours, the last thing Jamie needed was to see her office in shambles. However, it was too good a chance to catch Lys to turn down. "Okay," he said. "We'll be there soon as we can."

Returning to the bedroom, he woke Jamie and told her about the call as they dressed. Once they were both decent and Mischa had been let out, they were on their way.

"I didn't know freaky Lys was a runner," he commented as he negotiated the night-dark road.

"Five miles every weekday, seven to ten on weekends. She's really serious about it."

"Apparently, she's really serious about a lot of things." He checked his cell phone, saw it had no signal, then turned his attention back to the road. About halfway to the highway, they passed two armed guards, sitting on the tailgate of a Calloway truck, rifles in one hand, cigarettes in the other. Around the last curve before the highway, they reached the other two guards, similarly occupied. Both men raised a hand in greeting when they recognized Russ's truck.

As soon as he turned onto the road, the cell's signal strength went to maximum. He called Tommy, expecting to drag him out of bed or maybe catch him in the middle of his morning run, but Tommy was wide-awake and wasn't out of breath. There was a lot of noise in the background—shouts, the slow wail of a siren winding down, some sort of crackling.

"I've been trying to reach you," Tommy said.

"There's a dead zone on the road out here. What's up?"

"Someone set Jamie's house on fire. It's fully involved. Don't think they're gonna be able to save anything. And about a minute ago they got a call to another fire, this one on Calhoun Street. Lys's duplex. *Damn.*" Tommy's last word was followed by a crash so loud that Jamie, across the seat, flinched.

Russ could imagine the scene: fire trucks and police cars, their lights flashing in the dawn, neighbors standing around in robes or hastily thrown-on clothes, flames devouring everything in their path, brick and mortar collapsing into rubble.

But Jamie was safe. That was all that mattered.

"Lys called," Russ said shortly. "Said Jamie's office has been trashed and she wants Jamie to come in."

"So you go in to check it out, get surprised by the stalker, one or both of you get killed, and Lys discovers your bodies later this morning."

"Sounds about right. We're just coming into town. Why don't we meet someplace?"

"What? You don't want to face her alone?" Tommy teased.

"I'm not a cop," Russ retorted. "I'm not paid to deal with nutcases."

"I hear some of those people you build houses for can get pretty psycho. Meet me at the doughnut shop. I'm on my way." The sound of a gunning engine confirmed that an instant before the line went dead.

Russ set the phone on the seat beside him, then glanced at Jamie. He wasn't good at gently breaking news to anyone. When he'd returned from spring break that last year of law school, his first stop had been Jamie's apartment. She'd been looking pretty ragged from her bout of illness, and he'd said hello, how do you feel, then blurted out the words. *I met a girl, and we're getting married the week after graduation.*

Now he was just as blunt. "She set your house on fire."

Jamie's eyes widened, and she jerked around to look to the right. The sky had lightened enough to show plumes of dark smoke rising in the west, with occasional glimpses of a yellowish glow through the trees. Mouth open, she looked back at him, trying to speak but unable to put a thought together. "But— She— Why?"

"She set her house on fire, too. And what do you want to bet that she plans to burn the office, too, with me in it?"

Jamie's shoulders sagged, and suddenly she looked very tired, very fragile. Russ wanted to keep driving through the town and on into the day. He wanted to pull over and put his arms around her and hold her until she was strong again, to protect her from any more hurt or betrayal. But he made the turn for the doughnut shop, pulling into the parking lot where Tommy's SUV and three marked units were waiting.

Five minutes later, Jamie, still shaken and pale, got into Tommy's vehicle with him. Russ left the parking lot first, driving the few blocks downtown, turning at the square, taking the next right and parking in front of Jamie's building. Tommy and his officers stayed around the corner, out of sight.

Russ's palms were sweaty as he got out, touched Tommy's two-way radio in his pocket, locked in the transmit position, and crossed the sidewalk. His heart was beating a little too fast, his breaths coming a little shallow. Was this how Rick and Mitch felt when they started a new undercover assignment or found themselves face-to-face with the bad guys? They might thrive on the adrenaline rush, but not Russ. He just wanted life to go back to dull and boring. Just him and Jamie doing ordinary things—working, making love, making a home and a family.

He went inside the building, down the hall, then turned into the office. The first thing he noticed was the faint whiff of gasoline. He'd guessed right about one thing.

There was no sign of Lys immediately, but her words had certainly been true. The furniture had been tossed about, the cushions slashed open. Damaged books littered the floor, and the contents of the desk drawers had been dumped. The computer lay in pieces, and great gouges marked the walls. Even the carpet had been sliced in a fit of rage.

A noise came from Jamie's office—a soft pant—and he slowly, cautiously walked that way. The gasoline odor was stronger there; from the doorway, he saw the spout of a five-gallon can showing behind the overturned desk. The damage was the same as outside. Large sections of carpet were hidden under piles of paper from the file room, and Jamie's law degree lay in pieces around the room. Even the potted plant that had stood in the corner was destroyed, yanked from its pot, leaves stripped off.

Behind the desk, next to the gas can, stood Lys. She wore black jeans and a black T-shirt, and her hair was disheveled, her normally pale face red with exertion. Her eyes were glittering with excitement, anticipation, fury, and *he* was her target.

"Where's Jamie?" she demanded.

"She's still pretty weak. I left her at home." He wished he could have. If he could have let her rest, come out and dealt with this, then gone home to tell her that it was all over… But how could he have left her when there was a chance Lys was just trying to lure him away so *she* could get to her?

He moved a few steps farther into the room. "You usually jog in black jeans and a black shirt before dawn?" he asked mildly. "It's a wonder someone hasn't run you down." A pity, too. He waited a moment before he flatly stated, "She's in love with me, you know."

She shook her head so vehemently that the ends of her hair slapped her cheeks. "No. She's just emotional. Infatuated. She loves *me*. She said so."

He shook his head, too, slower, more emphatically. "She's been in love with me a long time. What she feels for you is friendship. That's all she'll ever feel for you."

Now her entire body was shaking. "No. No, she just thinks… It's this whole rescuer-victim thing. It wasn't supposed to work out this way. You weren't supposed to screw things up."

"You're the one who screwed things up. You stalked her. You drugged her dog. You scared her."

"It wasn't like that! I was—I was flirting with her. The note, the candy, the roses…they were just sweet little gifts. Having a secret admirer is fun, it's sexy. It's nothing to be scared of!"

Russ took a step and glass crunched beneath his feet. He glanced down and saw a photograph of Jamie with her family. It had been taken at a sister's wedding, and Jamie looked so happy. So carefree. "You *drugged* her dog."

Lys's expression turned mutinous. "She was watching you, thinking about you, remembering… I saw the look on her face. I knew she thought she still cared about you. She didn't, of course. She was just confused. Besides, Mischa was never at risk. It was just a sedative. I made sure the dose was right for her size."

"You put the tack strip under her tire."

Lys shrugged jerkily. "A flat. No big deal. It wasn't even her car. And it was a good plan. She would back out, her tire would go flat, and I'd come around the corner, headed home with her favorite pizza. Then you showed up and ruined it. You ruined everything. I was on my way to her house the next night to help her take Mischa to the vet, but you were there. When Tommy suggested she stay someplace else, she was supposed to come to *my* house, but you had already persuaded her to go home with you. You ruined it all!"

What was her plan now? He would have bet on a sneak attack—both times she'd caught Jamie off-guard. Given his size and the fact that he was inherently stronger than her, waiting behind the door with a baseball bat seemed more her style.

Then she moved, pulling a pistol from beneath her T-shirt, pointing it at him, her hand shaking violently. Jesus. Was this how Rick and Mitch felt when they knew odds were good they could die in the next few minutes? Probably not. If they ever got as scared as he was at that moment, they'd turn in their badges and take up fishing for a living.

He swallowed hard and forced a breath into his lungs. He didn't want to die here. He had too many reasons to live, starting and ending with Jamie. He'd wasted too much time being pissed off and hurt, and he wanted to make up for that. He wanted to die at a ripe old age with Jamie holding his hand.

He swallowed again. "Tommy knows it's you, Lys. He'll never let you get away with killing me, and Jamie will never forgive you for it."

Her agitation increased. "It doesn't matter now. Don't you see? Nothing matters now because of you! We had a chance. I know we did! And then you…"

From the corner of his eye, he gauged the distance between him and the door. Five, maybe six feet back and to his right. Whether he could make it would depend on how good a shot she was. The way she was trembling should count to his advantage, but the only thing worse than a competent person with a gun, Granddad used to say, was an incompetent one.

Where the hell was Tommy? Surely they'd heard enough by now. It was past time for them to come busting into the room, but he hadn't heard even a whisper of sound from outside.

"You won't even have her friendship anymore, Lys," he said, easing one step closer to the door.

"I know," she said softly. "But you won't have her, either. And she'll be sorry. She'll regret the choices she made. She'll realize that I really was the best thing that ever happened to her. She tells me that, you know. That she loves me. That meeting me was her lucky day."

Her face screwed up and tears filled her eyes.

"She lies. She loves you, she doesn't know what she would do without you—she's lying. She says the same things to me, and she didn't mean them. She never meant them." Angrily, she wiped her free hand across her face, and the other hand, the one with the gun, grew steadier. "She'll be sorry when we're dead."

Russ swallowed hard again. So much for using threat of arrest to sway her. He took another step back, but the crunch of glass underfoot brought her attention to what he was doing. She cocked the hammer on the pistol, leveled it square on his chest and snarled, "Stay where you are. Don't move—"

The gunshot was deafening in the confines of the office. For an instant, everything about him froze—no breath, no thought, no emotion—as he watched Lys's body jerk backward, thrown against the wall by the force of the blast. An instant later Tommy stepped into the room, his weapon in hand, and said quietly, "Funny. That's what I was about to say. You all right?"

Russ nodded. It would be a surprise if he made it outside without his legs giving way under him, but he was okay. He wasn't going to die, not today at least. Jamie was safe and waiting for him outside— No, she was shaking off the cop who tried to stop her at the door. Tears glittered in her eyes as she wrenched free, then hurtled across the room, throwing herself into his arms.

His legs weren't as weak as he thought. He caught her without staggering back more than a step or two and held her tightly, his face buried in her hair.

After a moment, she forced his head back, her hands cupped to his cheeks, and stared into his face. "Oh my God, Russ! She was going to kill you, and I'd never even told you I love you. I was so—" She swallowed. "Are you all right?"

Lys had been shot. Jamie's house and office had been destroyed. Her life was still in chaos, and as long as her life was, so was his. There would be statements to give, cleanups to start, all the hassles that came with vandalism and arson and attempted murder and criminal trials.

But he was alive, and the woman he loved had just said she loved him back. The rest of it paled to insignificance in the face of that.

"I'm better than all right," he told her, gently touching the uninjured side of her face. "I'm damn fine."

She smiled faintly. "And that's good?"

He smiled, too. "You and me together, James, for the rest of our lives…that's as good as it gets."

Epilogue

Jamie gazed at the ruins of her house, still smoldering in the morning light. She couldn't imagine the belonging that could have survived such heat. Everything—brick, concrete, steel—lay in a careless tumble, and sooty odor filled the air.

She sighed, and Russ, standing behind her, tightened his arms around her middle. "I know a great builder. He can replace this with anything your heart desires."

Her heart desired a lot, and in the past twenty-four hours, she'd gotten a lot. Russ was alive and well, Lys was under guard in the hospital, and the danger was past. Better, Russ had told her he loved her. Wanted her. Wanted babies with her. Yep, that was as good as it got.

Smiling, she turned in his arms to face him. "Actually, I've got my eye on a house north of town. Two years old, tough to find, but worth the effort."

"I know the place. It's not for sale."

"Oh, I don't want to buy it. I just want to share it."

His grin was charming. "There are some stiff requirements—marriage, a family, the rest of our lives."

"I think I can meet those." She moved so close that his breath was warm on her skin and murmured, "I have a stiff requirement or two of my own."

Right there, where anyone could see, he slid his hands to her hips and pulled her snug against him. "My requirements aren't negotiable. They're hard and fast."

"Funny. So are mine." She brushed her mouth across his. "And slow and easy, and always, always fine."

He kissed her, making her breath catch and her head spin, making everything right. Six years ago she had dreamed of so much with this man, and then he'd gone off and fallen in love with someone else, married someone else. But things happened in their own time, and six years ago hadn't been their time. They'd needed to grow, to each become the person the other couldn't live without.

Ending the kiss, he gazed at her for a time, his expression intense, then smiled. "Let's go home, James."

She let him lead her toward the truck, where she glanced back at the rubble of her house.

They'd survived their trial by fire. She didn't expect everything to be easy from now on.

But she damn sure expected it to be fine.

* * * * *

millsandboon.co.uk Community

Join Us!

The Community is the perfect place to meet and chat to kindred spirits who love books and reading as much as you do, but it's also the place to:

- **Get the inside scoop from authors about their latest books**
- **Learn how to write a romance book with advice from our editors**
- **Help us to continue publishing the best in women's fiction**
- **Share your thoughts on the books we publish**
- **Befriend other users**

Forums: Interact with each other as well as authors, editors and a whole host of other users worldwide.

Blogs: Every registered community member has their own blog to tell the world what they're up to and what's on their mind.

Book Challenge: We're aiming to read 5,000 books and have joined forces with The Reading Agency in our inaugural Book Challenge.

Profile Page: Showcase yourself and keep a record of your recent community activity.

Social Networking: We've added buttons at the end of every post to share via digg, Facebook, Google, Yahoo, technorati and de.licio.us.

www.millsandboon.co.uk